THE GH(O)ST ARMY DIARY

DEREK MILLER

LJ EMORY
PUBLISHING

LJ EMORY
PUBLISHING

Copyright © 2015 by Derek Miller

First L. J. Emory Publishing trade paperback edition June 2015

For information about special discounts for bulk purchases, please contact L. J. Emory Publishing, sales@ljemorypublishing.com

Manufactured in the United States of America

10 9 8 7 6 5 4 3 2

Library of Congress Control Number

2015907921

ISBN 978-1-940283-17-3
ISBN 978-1-940283-18-0 (ebook)

To my favorite brothers Caleb and Jacob. Who, like the Ghost Army, are there protecting me and watching out for me even when I don't see them or even know they are there.

CHAPTER ONE

"What am I going to do with you?" Judge Robert Hayes asked. "This is your third time in court!"

Becky didn't bother to give the judge a response. Instead, she hung her head and stared at the courtroom floor. She knew she wasn't a bad person, but here she was yet again. How had this happened? She'd made herself a solemn vow that she would never find herself in this position again, but . . . well . . . at fifteen it was hard to keep a vow like that. Especially when there was nothing to do and nowhere to go. Home was not a place she wanted to be.

The judge stared at her across his giant desk. Not with a look of disgust or pity but with a look that said he was concerned but frustrated with her. Becky had seen the same look on the face of her teachers several times before she stopped going to school. She had also seen that look on a couple of city street cops who, unfortunately, knew her by sight.

"Only a month ago, you gave me your solemn promise that I would not see you in here again, but here you are back in court for the destruction of public property," the judge said. "Would you care to explain how that happened?"

Becky had no idea how to explain her behavior to the judge. She couldn't even explain it to herself. Instead, she glanced up at the judge and thought about how to explain the compulsion she felt to draw or paint on any blank surface she could find.

That compulsion was the first thing she could remember. It had been there almost before she was old enough to hold a crayon.

In fact, even now her fingers itched to sketch this man in front of her who was waiting for an explanation. Judge Hayes was not a young man. His skin was starting to wrinkle and his eyes looked weary, as though he had seen too much during his years as a judge. He was still powerfully built and held himself erect as he sat behind the tall desk. Becky had heard rumors on the streets that this particular judge had been some kind of military hero a lifetime ago.

If only she had some decent supplies and a few minutes without having to respond to him. She would like to paint the judge—try to capture on canvas the stern kindness she saw hidden behind those eyes. That is, she could capture it if she had a canvas and some quality paints. It was hard getting her hands on decent artist supplies when she didn't have any money. In fact, this last transgression had come for no other reason than because she'd stumbled upon a bunch of leftover spray paint in a dumpster and couldn't bear not to use it.

"I'm still waiting for an answer." The judge drummed his fingers on his desk.

Becky shook herself out of the memory of how it had felt making the side wall of the city building come alive one night with the leftovers she'd rescued from the dumpster.

"It really wasn't destruction, your Honor," Becky argued. "I was just decorating that boring brick wall."

"Yes, but the boring brick wall happens to be the wall to one of our most important buildings." The judge's lips twitched slightly with amusement. "The mayor did not appreciate you spray painting a picture of him on a skateboard, kissing the back of a donkey's rear-end!"

From behind her, Becky heard other young people waiting their turn in the court room chuckle. This gave her the courage to plead her case a little further.

"He deserved it, your Honor. The mayor closed down

our skating park and I thought it might be a good idea to let him know we didn't appreciate it."

There was a light smattering of applause behind her.

"I'm sure he got your message loud and clear," the judge said, "but the damage you caused will cost the city about ten thousand dollars to clean up. That was old stone and it is a costly process to remove the paint from it. Do you happen to have ten thousand dollars lying around to reimburse the city?"

Ten thousand dollars? It might as well be ten million. Becky couldn't even afford to buy the thirty-five dollar sable-hair paint brush she'd been eyeing at the art store. It would have been an easy item to steal, but she had resisted the urge. At least for now.

"The mayor has recommended that I send you to the South Central Ohio Juvenile Detention Center in Chillicothe, Ohio, until you are 18 years old."

"For painting a wall?" Becky's eyes widened. That would be three years in jail!

"For defacing government property."

"But it was just a painting, your Honor," she pleaded. "I didn't mean any harm."

Judge Hayes leaned back in his chair as though considering his options. No one in the courtroom made a sound. The judge was known to be fair but stern.

"Please, sir . . ." Becky waited, her heart pounding hard while she tried to pretend to herself that she was tougher than she was.

"Ten-minute recess," Judge Hayes said abruptly. "You stay where you are, Becky. Don't move. I need to make a couple of phone calls before I make a ruling."

It was closer to fifteen minutes before the judge came back into the courtroom. Becky found it hard to breathe as she watched the seconds click away on the large clock on the wall.

"I just spoke to a friend with whom I graduated from West Point," Judge Hayes said. "He owes me a favor. I've arranged for you to spend the rest of the summer with his family and him in Mississippi. If you stay on your best behavior, his wife and he will give you a job. If they are happy with your work and with your attitude, I will postpone your sentencing. However, if you are so much as five minutes late waking up in the morning, I'll have you in the first police car going to the detention facility." He waited a beat to allow this to set in. "Or I can go ahead and send you to the detention facility now. The choice is yours."

Becky had no idea what was waiting for her in Mississippi, but she figured anything was better than going to juvenile jail. The judge was giving her a chance, and she grabbed it.

CHAPTER
TWO

Becky sat by the window of the Amtrak train watching the countryside whiz by. Next to her was the court-assigned escort who was supposed to take her from Chicago to Jackson, Mississippi. Becky was trying hard not to get her hopes up—but there was a tickle of excitement in her heart no matter how hard she tried to act nonchalant.

She replayed the judge's words after he had asked her to approach the bench. The judge had put his hand over the microphone that normally recorded everything he said. Then he'd said in a soft voice, "Becky, this truly is a once in a life time opportunity. Don't tell anyone, but I loved your artwork. The only criticism I have of it is you might have been a little too kind to the mayor. He's a lot uglier than you painted him."

Then the judge had winked, taken his hand off the microphone, and said in his stern voice, "Next case, please."

Becky was given a day to gather up her belongings although she could have done it in fifteen-minutes. She had nothing except a few clothes she put in a grocery shopping bag. Her foster parents were a little surprised that she was leaving, but they didn't act like they particularly cared. They didn't bother to hug her goodbye. Of course, hugs had been rare in Becky's world. She would have been surprised had they shown any affection or regret that she was leaving. Another foster kid would fill the void she'd left. There were always plenty of throwaways to go around.

At fifteen, she had pretty much raised herself. She'd been dropped off at a gas station when she was only two or three. The teenage clerk had called the police who transferred her to children services. She'd been in and out of foster homes ever since. Some of the homes had been toxic. Some had been just plain dangerous. Some had been neutral at best. She'd spent a lot of time crashing on couches at friends' houses, sometimes even sleeping in abandoned homes, etc. She'd learned to fight like a tiger if someone tried to lay a finger on her. Several years earlier, she'd started hanging around gangs and skateboard kids. There was at least some protection in numbers. It was with one of the gangs that she'd learned she had a knack for tagging or graffiti.

She'd started getting noticed on the streets for her "art" right before she started getting caught. All those stupid surveillance camera's made it more and more difficult to get away with things.

"Judge Hayes must really see something in you." Debbie, the court-appointed officer who was escorting her; closed the magazine she was reading and slipped it into her purse. "I've never seen him do this for anyone else."

"I hope you're right," Becky said, "but don't they just play banjos and grow cotton down there in Mississippi?"

"I'm sure there's a lot more to that state than that," Debbie said. "I do know it's hot in the summer and they have lots of fire ants."

"What are fire ants?"

"From what I've heard, you don't want to get near them. Still . . . if I were you, I'd rather be bit by a hundred of them than face Judge Hayes if you blow this opportunity he's given you."

"Do you have any idea what this friend of the judge's is like?" Becky was nervous about being so far away from her usual haunts and street friends. What would she do if this situation turned bad? Where could she go?

"I don't have a clue," Debbie said. "He's never done this before for any other case I've seen him work with."

Then Debbie reclined her seat and closed her eyes. The hypnotizing effect of the passing scenery eventually put Becky to sleep as well. It had been an emotionally draining two days, and she was grateful that Debbie didn't seem to want to chat.

With a jolt the train came to a stop at the Jackson Train Station which woke them up. As they disembarked onto the platform, Becky saw one person there—a tall man wearing a cowboy hat.

If this was the judge's friend, there was a small problem with this picture. Becky was white. She had plenty of black friends back home, but it seemed strange to her that the judge would place her with a black family.

"Are you Rusty?" Debbie asked.

"Yes, ma'am," he said. "That's what they call me."

"This is the girl the judge sent down to you," Debbie said. "Her name is Becky."

"Good to meet you, Becky," Rusty shook her hand. "Are you ready to leave? My wife is in the car and we have about an hour's drive to get home."

Debbie officially checked Rusty's I.D. and had him sign some paperwork. He offered to drop off Debbie at the local hotel where she could stay the night, but she declined and took a taxi. Becky was a bit sad for her to go because she was the last thing connecting her to Chicago.

Once they arrived at the car, Rusty's wife jumped out and Becky saw that she was lovely.

"I'm so sorry I couldn't meet you at the platform, but I

was on a conference call and couldn't hang up." Then she gave Debbie a big hug. "Welcome to Mississippi, sweetie. I think you're going to like it here."

Becky was not used to hugs and tried not to have much physical contact with anyone. She did not return the hug, but Rusty's wife didn't seem to notice.

"I'm Claire and I'm honored you will be staying with us this summer!"

"An honor?" Becky said; "You do know that I was sent here by Judge Hayes, right? It was either you or going to jail."

"Minor technicality," Claire gave a dismissive wave of her hand. "Just a minor technicality. If the Judge saw fit to send you down here then there must be something very special about you."

Rusty opened the trunk of the car, took the bag out of Becky's hands and placed it inside.

"Me and Robert Hayes go way back. We served together during the Iraqi war—the first one."

They put Becky in the back seat and pulled out of the parking lot.

"Where are we going?" Becky asked.

"To a small town called Kosciusko, Mississippi. I'm sure you've never heard of it, but we are famous for one thing—

being the birthplace of Oprah Winfrey!" He chuckled. "Aren't you excited?"

"To be honest, I didn't even know Jackson, Mississippi, existed until I saw my train ticket there, let alone this Kosci—whatchamacallit where you live."

"Kosciusko," Rusty said, "but we usually just call it home."

"What will I be doing?" Becky asked.

"Oh, a little of this and a little of that," Rusty said. "We have a small farm that we run; plus, we operate a camouflage plant."

The idea of living on a farm was so alien to Becky that she didn't know how to even feel about it. All she knew of farms were some pictures she'd seen in books. Until today, she'd never been outside the city limits of Chicago.

"Camouflage plant?" she asked, focusing on the thing that most intrigued her. Did that involve painting?

"Oh. we make outfits for hunters and military that help them blend into their environment," Rusty said. "Be it snow, desert, forest, fields, mountains, etc, we can hide anyone. We are small town but we're pretty high tech."

"Interesting." Becky wondered if Rusty and Claire had any video games at their house.

"Honey," Claire said, "I know you're nervous and this is all new and different but relax. Yes, you are going to work hard this summer but the judge did not send you to do nothing but work. He told us he thinks you need some real family exposure and to get out of the city. He tells us you're pretty quick with a paint brush, so first thing tomorrow morning, we have some walls in desperate need of a coat of paint if you don't mind using a roller instead of a brush. Does that sound like a plan you'd approve?"

"Yeah." Becky responded with a slightly embarrassed smile, "I'm pretty good with paint."

CHAPTER THREE

The next morning Becky woke up disorientated. That happened to her a lot. She rarely found herself in the same place twice if she could help it, so it always took her a few seconds to figure out where she was.

She finally remembered she was in Mississippi and why. The wall clock said it was ten after seven. She did not quite know what to do with herself, so she dressed, quietly opened the door, and walked out. She heard noises coming from the kitchen and went in.

Claire was pouring some orange juice while Rusty was seated at the table reading the paper. It was obvious he had been out running by the looks of his sweat drenched t-shirt and shorts.

"Good morning, city girl," Rusty said. "You sleep well?"

"I guess."

"Sit down and let's get some breakfast in you, girl." Claire said.

Becky sat down. She was not used to waking up to a real breakfast. Claire handed her a plate heaped with fruit, bacon and eggs.

"You think that will hold you for now?" Claire said with a grin. "I remember being your age. My mama said she thought she'd never get me filled up."

Becky was starved and started wolfing it all down.

"Eat all you want," Rusty said. "You're going to need your energy. Starting tomorrow you're going to start running with me in the morning."

Becky didn't know what to say other than, "Okay." She was not afraid of running. She had run from cops, other adults, and teens who had wanted to hurt her. She was good at running but not necessarily the kind she thought Rusty was talking about.

"Rusty, don't scare the poor thing," Claire said. "She just got here."

"Fresh morning air never hurt anyone," Rusty said. "Guess it is time for me to get a shower, drop by and see Dad, and get to work."

With that Rusty excused himself from the table and left the room.

Once it was just the two of them, Claire said, "Honey,

I know this is not the summer you picked for yourself, but if you work with us, we will work with you. My Rusty is a good man and I can't wait for you to meet his father. I think you will find him the most interesting of us all. He is in the veterans home about two miles from here and we visit him every day. That is one thing you will be helping with this summer. Dad's health is bad, eye sight even worse, and he loves to listen to people read. Do you think you would be okay with doing that?"

Becky gave it some thought.

"I've never visited a veterans home but reading to your dad shouldn't be a problem." Becky smiled as she said this. She knew that Claire had no idea how easy anything she'd mentioned sounded. With food this good and people this kind, the summer was going to be a breeze.

Claire smiled back. "Now you get out of my kitchen, go to your room and make a list of things you need like a toothbrush, tennis shoes, clothes, etc. I'll clean up and then we'll go to town and get you all set for a summer in Mississippi."

CHAPTER FOUR

"This is all?" Claire stared at the list Becky had written. "A pair of jeans and a shirt? Some toothpaste and soap?"

Becky nodded. She didn't want to be a burden. She'd whittled her original list down to the bare bones.

"Honey," Claire said, "we can get you more than that. How about some running shoes? Nail polish? Shampoo? It isn't possible for you to have everything a teenage girl needs in that small bag you brought with you. I know you need more."

"I didn't want to ask for more," Becky answered truthfully. "You and Rusty are already doing enough."

"Maybe so but not enough for Judge Hayes. He saved my husband's life. Did he tell you that?"

"No."

"Taking care of you, buying you a few clothes—well,

it's small potatoes to pay back what Judge Hayes did for us. Besides that . . . I like you and I enjoy having you here. You're no bother, honey."

It struck Becky that this was the single kindest thing anyone had ever said to her. She'd spent most of her life feeling like a bother to the overworked social workers, the foster parents, the cops. Hearing someone as nice as Claire say that she was enjoying having her around and actually liked her . . . Becky had to fight back sudden tears, but she did manage to keep from breaking down. It was early days. She would see how Claire felt a week from now or a month. People didn't always show their true selves all at once. She'd learned it was best to be cautious.

Claire was as good as her word though. She made sure that Becky got some extra shirts, pants, a comb, some nail polish, a pair of running shoes, etc. Every essential a teen girl would need. She even called a friend whose daughter had left for college and had left much of her closet of clothes behind. They stopped by and got even more outfits that were Becky's size. It was the first time Becky had ever had anything without a hole or a rip in it.

Next they stopped by the "Camo" office. Becky was taken aback. She was picturing some run down factory, but when Claire and Rusty started giving her a tour, she was blown away by how clean and new it looked. Fabric was going every direction but the floors were spotless, and those working the machines smiled and greeted her. Each took the time to explain to Becky what they did from cutting, sewing, designing, etc.

She visited the shipping area and the high tech computer room where they were always coming up with new styles and designs, etc.

"So, what do you think?" Rusty asked after Claire and he had shown her the entire place and then took her to the cafeteria where he ordered milkshakes for all three of them. "Are you impressed with our family business?"

"Yes," she said. "It's so much bigger than I ever dreamed. How did you start all this?"

"Dad started it right after he came back from the war. He had a real knack for designing new styles. Camouflage is mainly purchased by the military and hunters, and they liked the things he designed for them. Special camo for turkey hunting, for instance. Well-constructed clothing that would blend into every kind of environment. It wasn't long until he was designing stuff to be sent all over the world. I never understood it. He was just a clerk in London but he just had this skill to be able to hide people like never before."

"Could he make something for me to wear that would blend in with concrete and brick buildings?" Becky laughed. "I do have some experience trying to hide in Chicago."

"I know you're making a joke," Claire said, "but that's exactly the kind of thing that Rusty's dad could have done back when he was younger. He was amazing. Thank goodness, Dad taught Rusty well before he started losing his eyesight and we can afford to hire designers now."

"I'm looking forward to meeting him," Becky said.

Rusty and Claire shared a glance. "We'll see if you still feel that way afterward," Rusty said. "Dad can be . . . a little difficult these days."

"In what way?"

"You'll see," Claire said. "Now, we need to get back to the house and get all your new clothes put away. You've got some other work to help me with for the next few days. Then Rusty wants you to help down here a little and learn what you can and after that we'll schedule you a time to read to Dad."

Becky found herself worrying a bit about reading to the old man now—especially after that worried look between Claire and Rusty. How bad could reading to an old veteran be?

CHAPTER
FIVE

Becky had never had a room all to herself before and she enjoyed the fact that she now had a bedroom to call her own. It was quite plain, and the white walls called to her to decorate them with color, but she tried to ignore the urge. This was not her house and she would not deface the home in which she had been treated so well.

A few days into her stay, Claire surprised her with a suggestion that they make a trip to the paint store together.

"Why?" Becky asked.

"Your room," Claire answered. "I've always wanted a mural on one of our walls, but good mural painters are hard to find and expensive. Would you like to give it a try?"

Becky felt her heart give a jump of joy. She could hear from the sound in Claire's voice that she was serious. "What kind of a mural?"

"Anything you want," Claire said. "Something that will make you happy every time you walk into that bedroom."

Becky quickly thought through all the various scenarios. She couldn't be sure until she could get her hands on some paper and a pencil, but an idea began to form.

"Could I have a sketch pad?" she asked. "It doesn't have to be expensive or anything, but I'll need to work the design out on it first."

"Let's gather up everything you might need here at the paint store and then we'll go to the local hobby store. They'll have everything else."

Rusty helped her move all of the furniture out of her bedroom later on that evening. For a week, Becky kept the door to her bedroom closed and slept on the twin bed he'd placed in the living room. The thing that amazed her was that neither Rusty nor Claire seemed annoyed at having their living room temporarily turned into the storage area for the bedroom furniture. Instead, they seemed excited and curious about what she was doing on the walls behind the door she kept shut. Neither seemed to worry that they would not like what she was painting.

At first, it felt like a lot of responsibility and then as she got further into the project, the worry of doing well fell away, and she became obsessed with the picture she was trying to create. Hours would melt away and she would forget to eat. Claire would politely knock on the door and when Becky would open it, there would be a tray of food and Claire would have disappeared. Toward the end of the week, Becky became so excited, she could hardly sleep. Never before had she been given freedom, the tools, and the privacy to do something like this. She would eat her sandwich sitting cross-legged in the middle of the bedroom floor and appraise what she'd done and make decisions about what else she needed to do.

Finally, when she'd placed the last brush stroke, she stepped back swelling with pride as she decided that the mural was one of her greatest accomplishments. She crawled into bed and slept for twelve straight hours. When she awoke, there was sunlight streaming through the living room windows and Claire and Rusty were talking softly in the kitchen while they had breakfast.

As she walked in, Claire jumped up. "You've been asleep forever. We were starting to get worried. Can I fix you something to eat?"

"Not yet," Becky said. "Would you like to see what I've done?"

She had no idea how they would react. All she knew was that she'd put her heart and soul onto those walls.

Becky stood behind them so she would not block their view, and so it was not possible to see their faces—but when she heard them gasp she knew that they were impressed. They stood there in silence for a long time as though trying to take it all in.

"Are you sure you're only fifteen?" Rusty asked. "This is a masterful work."

She waited. Claire, without saying a word turned around, tears pooling in her eyes and with a big smile she embraced Becky. Then with her arm around Becky's shoulders, all three turned to gawk at the painting again.

"The detail!" Rusty said.

"The emotional impact!" Claire said.

Becky knew then that she'd done a good job. She had deliberately painted the bottom half of the four walls a light charcoal. That would look good against the white wooden bedroom furniture she had. The upper half was where she had let herself go.

It was a city scene she had painted. Chicago, with every building as accurate as possible. There were people in the painting, a small child sitting on a doorstep petting a dog, a mother with a stroller, an elderly man in a wheel chair. There were street people, beggars, and a drug pusher peering around a corner hiding from a cop. There were gang members leaning against a brick wall acting cool, and there were various gang signs on some of the buildings. A derelict church was in one corner, and there was just enough trash blowing along the street to make the scene look authentic. It was the inner city. Her home. The place she knew like the back of her hand. Had Rusty or Claire asked, she could have told them each person's name that she'd painted. They were real people. People she knew. Some she loved, some she was afraid of, and some she avoided. Some she'd helped. Some were white. More were black.

"Who is this?" Claire pointed to a small lonely-looking white child standing in the furthest corner.

"That's me," Becky said.

"You?"

"That's me when I was about three."

"You look cold in that picture."

"I was."

Claire started to speak, and then didn't, but Becky knew there would be follow up questions. It surprised her to realize that if it was Claire asking them, she wouldn't mind so much giving the answers.

"Amazing," Rusty said shaking his head. "Absolutely amazing . . . but I have to get to work. Thank you for this, Becky. I'll help you move your furniture back in here tonight."

"I think it's time that I take Becky to see Dad," Claire said. "That is if you feel up to it, Becky."

"Oh, yes," Becky said. "I'm finished here. I'd be happy to do something different."

CHAPTER
SIX

While Becky took a quick shower and a hurried breakfast, Claire kept making trips back to the room to look at the painting. After Becky finished her breakfast, Claire and she went to the veterans home to visit Rusty's father.

It was a little bit of a letdown for Becky when she got there because the old man was asleep.

Claire looked at her watch. "I have to go. Would you mind staying here awhile? You can watch TV or read until he wakes up."

Becky looked around the room. She wasn't used to being around old people a whole lot but there didn't seem to be anything scary here. "Sure. I'll stay."

"Normally, I would stay and talk with him a bit, introduce you, and see if he needs anything, but I'm late for a meeting. I'll be back in two hours to pick you up."

With that, Claire left. Becky was reaching for the TV

remote on the bedside table when she saw Rusty's dad open one eye.

"Is she gone?" the old man whispered.

"Excuse me?" Becky said.

"Is that woman gone?"

"As far as I know," Becky said.

"Good!" The old man sat straight up in bed. "I love my daughter-in-law, but when she visits, she makes such a fuss it is downright embarrassing! Making sure I'm eating, making sure my pillow is fluffed, checking with the nurses to make sure I've taken all my medication. I'm only ninety years old, for goodness sake! I can look after myself!"

Becky bit her lip to keep from laughing.

He squinted at her then picked up a pair of glasses from the bedside table, stuck them on his nose and looked at her. "Why . . . you're a white girl I'm guessing!"

"I am."

"That probably means you're not one of my grandkids."

"Nope. I'm Becky. I'm supposed to read to you until Claire comes back."

"Read to me?" he said. "I don't want anybody reading to me. Why does Claire think I want to have someone reading to me? What I want is to go dancing!"

"Dancing?" Becky didn't know what to say. This old man was not at all what she had been expecting.

"Problem is, my legs don't work too good anymore." He squinted at her again. "What did you say your name is?"

"Becky."

"You sure you're not one of my grandkids?"

"I'm sure." She decided to take the conversation in another direction. "I don't know what your name is though. All I've heard Rusty and Claire call you is "Dad."

"My name?" He laid his head back against the bed. "You know, it's been so long since I was called anything but 'Dad' I can't remember my own name."

"Are you serious?" Becky asked. "You really can't remember your own name?"

"Of course, I can," the old man said, indignantly. "I'm not senile!"

"So what do I call you?"

He chuckled. "You can call me anything as long as you don't call me late for dinner."

Becky blew out a sigh. This was going to be tougher than she'd imagined.

"All right, all right," he said. "You can call me 'Granddad.' I like the sound of 'Granddad."

"Granddad it is, then," Becky said. "Do you want me to read to you or not?"

"Well," he said. "I guess I got nothing better to do."

CHAPTER
SEVEN

The old man had fallen asleep while Becky had been reading. At least she thought he was asleep. She stopped reading and laid the book Claire had given her down. It wasn't particularly interesting to her. Just a lot of dusty old history about World War II. Granddad had seemed interested in it though.

Granddad. She liked calling him that. She'd never had a grandfather and as crusty and cantankerous as he was, she liked him.

She glanced at the wall clock. She'd been reading for an hour. She had another hour to fill before Claire came back and she didn't really feel like watching TV.

A spiral notebook was sitting on the table with nothing written on it. A freshly sharpened pencil laid beside it. It was always hard for her to see a blank page without wanting to fill it with some of the pictures that were in her head, so she picked it up and started doodling. Before long the doodle began to take shape. There had been an old dog a few months back that she'd found in an abandoned yard. She had scrounged food for it and kept it fed until it got hit by a car and died. It had broken her heart at the time, but her heart had been broken so many times in her life that she'd simply forced herself to go on and not think about it too much. Now she tried to capture the grateful look in its eyes each time it saw her. She had been drawing for several minutes and was so focused she had not noticed that Granddad was awake and watching her.

He cleared his throat and she jumped.

"Oh, sorry," Becky closed the notebook quickly. "I didn't know you were awake."

"What are you doing?" he said.

"Oh, nothing," she said. "I'm just drawing a little to pass the time. I hope that's okay."

"You like to draw?" he said.

"I love to draw but sometimes it gets me into trouble."

"Trouble?"

"Sometimes I draw pictures where I'm not supposed to. That's why I'm staying with Claire and Rusty. The judge was supposed to send me to juvie but changed his mind and sent me to help out Claire and Rusty for the summer instead."

Granddad ignored that information. "Are you any good at drawing?"

"Some people think so."

"Let me see." Granddad held out his hand. "If you're here on my time and I'm paying you the big bucks, I want to see what you're drawing."

"You aren't paying me anything. I'm here because Claire brought me to read to you."

"Hmmm. I can see that some negotiation is necessary." The old man screwed up his face and pondered. "How about I give you my pudding today when lunch comes? It's supposed to be chocolate."

"You don't have to give me your pudding or pay me." She opened the notebook to the page she'd been working on and handed it to him. "I don't mind if you look at my drawing."

He held it close to his face and squinted. "Please hand me my glasses."

She obediently handed him the glasses he'd taken off right before he'd fallen asleep. He put them on and studied the drawing for a lot longer than she'd expected. It made her nervous.

"It's not very good," she said. "I was just passing the time."

Finally, he looked up at her and raised an eyebrow. His

cantankerous expression had disappeared. Instead, he was staring at her intently. "Who taught you?"

"What do you mean?" Becky asked.

"Who taught you how to draw?"

"No one, I just . . . draw."

At that moment they heard Claire's voice coming down the hallway. Granddad immediately threw the note pad back at Becky, jerked off his glasses and slammed his head back on the pillow where he pretended to be asleep.

Claire walked in and saw him. "He's still asleep?"

Becky decided not to tell on the old man. If he wanted to pretend in front of Claire it was no business of hers.

"Hello, Claire." A nurse walked in, "Time for your medicine, Mr. Evans. Wake up."

"Come on, Becky. It's time for us to go." Claire hesitated. "Although maybe we should stay until I know he has taken his medicine and . . ."

"Oh no." Becky jumped up. "Let's go ahead and get going. I'm sure he won't mind."

When Claire's back was turned to the door, Granddad looked up and gave her a big grin and a thumbs' up behind the nurse's back. It was all Becky could do to keep from rolling her eyes. What a stinker!

The last thing she heard as she and Claire walked down the hall was Granddad trying to sweet talk the nurse.

"Let's run away," he said. "I have money. We'll go to Tahiti together. We'll have a good life!"

"I would love to." There was a smile in the nurse's voice. "But I don't think my husband and four kids would approve."

"Great!" Granddad's enthusiasm wasn't the least bit dimmed. "We'll bring 'em all with us!"

CHAPTER
EIGHT

The next day when Claire and Becky walked in Granddad was awake and chatted awhile with Claire. He seemed to enjoy hearing how the business was doing and any other news. However, in Kosciusko the news didn't seem to change that often.

After Claire left, Granddad focused all his attention on Becky. "Draw me a picture."

"Of what?"

He gave it some thought. "How about drawing a typical park in Chicago?"

"There's nothing special about the parks in Chicago," Becky said. "Don't you want me to read to you instead?"

"Nope," Granddad said. "I don't want you to read. I've never been to Chicago and I want to know more about what it looks like. Take as long as you want. Don't do it on notebook paper this time. There's a sketch pad in my top drawer over there. Grab it instead."

Becky wondered why Granddad would have a sketch pad in his drawer, but she didn't question it. She got it out, sat down close to his bed where he could watch over her shoulder and started to draw. As she did, Granddad put on his glasses and watched her hand movements carefully. To her surprise, Granddad didn't interrupt her or ask any questions. He just let her draw.

Finally, she said, "I could go on forever, but I'm done for now."

Granddad reached for the drawing, looked at it closely, and sighed. "Are you sure you're only fifteen?"

"I'm pretty sure."

He glanced up at her. "Pretty sure?"

She hesitated. It was something she rarely talked about.

"I once saw the newspaper article of the story about me being abandoned at a gas station twelve years ago," she answered. "They think I was about two or three. I use the newspaper date as my birthday."

A look of concern crossed Granddad's face, but Claire walked back in before he could say anything. It surprised her that enough time had elapsed for Claire to even be here. It seemed like she'd only started to draw five minutes ago, but when she glanced at the clock, she realized it had been over two hours.

It was always like that when she was drawing. Time just seemed to stand still.

Claire saw what Becky had been doing. "Now, Dad," Claire said. "Becky is supposed to be reading to you."

"She's a better drawer than she is a reader," Granddad said. "I enjoyed watching her. The girl has talent."

"Well, maybe you can teach her a thing or two," Claire said.

"Do you draw?" Becky asked. "You didn't tell me that."

"I used to dabble around a little," he said.

"A little?" Claire said.

Granddad made a shooing gesture. "I'm tired. Bring this kid back again tomorrow, along with the biggest New York style pizza you can carry. I'm sick of pudding and jello."

CHAPTER
NINE

As Granddad had asked, Becky returned the next day but to his disappointment with no pizza. Claire was a stickler for following the doctor's strict dietary instructions. Becky picked up the history book to read, but once again he had a better plan.

"I want you to draw another picture today. It may be hard but I want you to try. Draw a picture of what it looked like the night you were dropped off at the gas station."

Becky was taken back. "I was only three."

He handed her the sketch pad she'd used the day before, which he'd been studying before she came in. "Doesn't matter. Use your imagination. Try."

"But . . ."

"I'm only asking you to try," Granddad said.

Becky stared at the blank sheet for a moment, and then her hand started sketching. Again she was lost in her own world. Granddad once again put on his glasses and watched every hand movement.

Finally, she was finished and handed it over. He took a lot of time studying it.

"I see your mother in the shadows of the gas station lights," he said. "You camouflaged her perfectly.

"I did hide her in the drawing," Becky said, "I've always thought that maybe she didn't really just abandon me. Maybe she stayed behind to make sure I was taken care of. Maybe she looked over me the best she could."

"I'm sure she did." Granddad's voice was soft. He laid the drawing in his lap, took off his glasses and rested his eyes. "You have no idea the reason why you are in this room with me, do you?"

"I thought I was here to read to you."

"Nope. I wondered why a young hooligan from Chicago was sent down here, but the reason is so unique, there is no other reason for it other than the Man upstairs made sure you made it here to me. I guess I still have something left that I need to do even if I am ninety years old."

"What do you mean?"

"I'm tired, Becky." Granddad said. "Tomorrow we'll talk about some things that might interest you, but right now I need to rest . . . and think."

CHAPTER
TEN

Becky was enjoying staying with Rusty and Claire more than she'd ever imagined possible. It felt safe at the house where they lived and she often took walks around the neighborhood. There was a sweet little boy next door, about five years old, who would sometimes come outside and ask her to play ball with him. His mother usually sat on the porch and read while they passed the ball back and forth. She was nice and sometimes brought cookies outside and thanked Becky for helping use up some of his energy.

Rusty had installed new carpeting in her room and it was the perfect color to go with her painting. Claire put up new curtains. It seemed like every time Claire went shopping, she brought home something else for Becky to wear, and it was always something pretty. Becky had never had so many clothes to choose from and every morning was like Christmas when she went to her closet and got to pick out something different instead of wearing the same thing day after day.

She was grateful for all the kindness that she was being shown, and she responded to it by helping with everything she could. She didn't know how to cook much, so she made a point of washing all the dishes after Claire put dinner on the table. At first Claire protested, but Becky was determined that Claire and Rusty go into the living room and let her take care of cleaning up the kitchen.

They had fallen into a sort of family-type routine. This was a new thing to her—this having a routine of any kind. After Rusty and she ran together, he would go to work and Claire and Becky would do a little housework or laundry. Then Claire would drop Becky off at Granddad's and take care of errands or go do bookwork at the camouflage factory. At night, after dinner, they would play board games or watch TV. Sometimes Rusty would play video games with her while Claire flipped through magazines.

Compared to all the years before, this summer felt like heaven to Becky. Her main job, which was keeping Granddad company for a couple hours each afternoon, didn't seem like a burden at all. She had begun to look forward to it. He wasn't at all senile like she'd thought the first day. Instead, she discovered that he just had a really great sense of humor and loved messing with people.

Except he didn't do that with her anymore. With her, he was serious and seemed to understand her obsession with drawing—which she'd thought of as a personal weakness. She always seemed to be getting into trouble over it. After all, she'd certainly been reprimanded enough times in school for decorating her test papers with drawings, while getting bad grades on those tests. There was also *graffiti* but that was a word the cops used to describe what she did. She saw it as decorating empty spaces on brick and concrete walls with art.

A week after she drew her mother standing in the shadows at the gas station, he surprised her with an unusual request.

"There is a black trunk in the closet," he said. "Go pull it out. Bring it here."

It was heavy, but Becky managed to drag it over to the bed. The box appeared to be very old. It had leather, metal hinges, and was shabby-looking.

"Now open it," he said.

The antique trunk definitely piqued her interest. She couldn't imagine what could be inside it that he wanted to show her.

"In the top of the trunk there is a little piece of ribbon sticking out," Granddad said. "Do you see it? It looks like a small clothing tag."

Becky saw the little piece of ribbon.

"I found it. Now what?"

"Pull on it," he said.

Once again Becky did what she was told. Suddenly, a secret compartment opened and out fell an oversized book with a leather band and lock on it. She gasped in surprise. She would never have guessed that there was a secret compartment in the old trunk. It was extremely well hidden and the book fit inside it perfectly.

"Close your mouth, girl," Granddad said. "You look like you're trying to catch flies."

She hadn't realized her mouth had fallen open. As she closed it, she looked up at him and saw that he had tears in his eyes.

"What's wrong, Granddad?" she asked.

"For fifty years what I did during the war was top secret." His voice trembled. "I've held onto those secrets too long. I've waited for the right person to come along to share them with. I prayed about it a long time last night, and I think the right person is you."

"But I'm only fifteen," she protested.

"I know," he said, kindly. "But you were born with an artist's heart. I think you'll understand better than most. Besides that, you are as bright as a new copper penny."

From around his neck he pulled a thin gold chain with

a tiny key. He handed the key to her. "Here, this will fit the book's lock."

She tried it and the key fit perfectly. She gently placed the book on the bed next to Granddad.

"This is my diary—my story." Granddad patted it gently. "I think it will be a lot more interesting to you than the history book Claire chose for you to read to me."

CHAPTER
ELEVEN

Becky had been so intent on Granddad's secret that she'd barely breathed since the moment he'd handed her the key. With no idea what she would discover, she took a deep breath and opened to the first page.

The front cover was blank except for the name "Jared Cline" written in neat block letters.

Jared Cline? Who was he? And what did he have to do with Granddad?

Then she turned the page and saw an amazing drawing of Times Square in New York City. She had never been to New York. She'd only seen it on TV on New Year's Eve, but as she took in every detail of the drawing, she felt like she was standing right in the middle of it—or at least how it might have looked sixty years earlier.

Granddad was silent as she gazed at the drawing. Finally, she looked at Granddad.

"Are you Jared Cline?"

"I used to be. Deep down I guess I still am."

"Did you draw this picture?" she asked.

"Yes," he responded. "Like you, I never had a lesson either."

He leaned back against the pillows of his bed, took his glasses off and rubbed his eyes. "I didn't sleep well last night. These are the words and pages of my life . . . and some of the memories written there will not be easy for you to read or for me to hear."

The words were written in the same neat, block writing that she'd seen on the first page—as though the person wielding the pen was making the writing itself a form of art.

The strangest thing happened today and I have a feeling I should start keeping a diary. It appears that there is to be an adventure in my future. Whether it will be hard or easy remains to be seen.

I've been working at a small ad agency for about a year now here in New York. One of my old bosses, Brian, who I only worked with for a few months showed up in full military uniform. He and I worked on a lot of projects together in the short time he was here. We made some pretty special ads that drew some attention. I knew he had served in the military but I thought he had done his time and had come home. I was wrong. He was still in the military, but had been reassigned. He walked straight in and stopped at my desk. His was frowning as though he were angry about something.

This worried me. I wondered if I was in trouble.

"Jared, do you have a minute?" he asked.

It isn't easy getting a job now, especially if you are a black man who makes his living as an artist. The serious sound of his voice was unlike him. He'd never acted like this before when we'd worked together. We were both creative people and making those ads together had felt like play. He liked to tell jokes, and I enjoyed hearing and laughing at them.

"Yes." I tried to keep the sound of fear out of my voice. "I have a minute."

"Good," he said. "Please follow me."

I followed him into the office of my current boss. As we entered, Brian politely asked my boss to leave us alone for a private talk. To my surprise, my boss didn't seem surprised or argue.

Instead, my boss just scooped up a pile of papers on his desk and left his own office.

"Sit down, Jared," Brian said.

I sat. I knew absolutely at this point I was going to be fired.

"What I'm about to say is top secret," Brian said. "If you tell anyone what I'm about to say, I'll hunt you down and put you in a prison that is so secret and far away no one will ever find you."

His words sounded so dramatic that I nearly laughed from sheer nerves. What could Brain tell me—an artist at an ad agency—that would be so top secret that I'd go to prison if I ever told?

Brian did not smile when he said this. The man was dead serious. I briefly wondered where the happy-go-lucky artist that I'd known before he joined the military had gone.

"I know your work, Jared. Probably better than anyone here. You are highly skilled, underappreciated and going nowhere at this agency."

Well, he had that right.

"That doesn't matter," I said. "My father taught me to be grateful for a job—any job—and to work hard. I appreciate getting a pay check."

Brian waved away my words as though he were waving away a cloud of gnats.

"I am helping put together a secret military unit unlike any that has ever been seen before and I want you to be part of it."

"But I've never fired a gun," I said. "Plus, my feet are flat and I can't march very far. I tried to volunteer after

Pearl Harbor, but the military said I wasn't in good enough shape to be a soldier."

"One part of this secret unit is going to be made up of artists," Brian said. "I want you on my team. Will you join with me to help beat the Nazis?"

CHAPTER
TWELVE

Becky could hardly contain herself the next day. She was dying to get back to Granddad and read more of his diary. Yesterday, she felt like she'd barely gotten started when Claire came to get her. Granddad had already fallen asleep by the time Claire arrived and he didn't seem to just be pretending to be asleep today. He seemed to genuinely be asleep. She wondered if he'd worn himself out just thinking about the events she'd been reading about.

During Rusty's and her run, she was so impatient to get to Granddad, she ran faster than she ever had. Even Rusty mentioned the speed with which they'd completed their two mile run.

"Wow, girl!" He bent over with his hands on his knees, trying to get his breath. "It's starting to be a challenge for me to keep up with you. When you get back to Chicago you should try out for your school's cross country team."

"I'll think about it," she said.

In fifteen minutes she had showered and was already out the door and sitting in the car waiting on Claire to drive her to the Veteran's home.

"Well, aren't you the early bird this morning," Claire said, as she fastened her seat belt and put her key into the ignition. "Are you certain you're the same girl we picked up at the train station a few weeks ago?"

As they drove Becky mentally tried to make Claire drive faster, but it wasn't working. This morning Claire had to go by the post office first and of course one of Claire's dear friends was there as well. Twenty minutes later, they were moving again at last. As they neared the veterans home, Becky told Claire that she didn't have to take the time to park the car. She suggested Claire just stop and let her out.

Claire gave her an odd look but pulled up to the entry and let Becky out under the portico.

"If Granddad needs anything," Claire called out the window, "call me on my cell."

"Sure will!" Becky waved and headed into the building that she was beginning to know well. She hoped Granddad was awake and alert enough for her to read more of the diary to him. There was so much she wanted to know about his story.

She needn't have worried. He was wide awake and flirting with the same nurse Becky had met the first day.

"Are you sure you don't want to run away to Tahiti with me?" he said. "I can be a lot of fun when I'm not in a hospital bed."

"You're fun enough." She patted his hand. "You don't need to go to Tahiti—although my husband says he appreciates the offer to take the kids and him along."

"You mean you told him about us and he wasn't jealous?" Granddad pretended to be shocked. "Did you tell him how handsome I am?"

"He said you sound like someone he'd like to meet," she said.

"Your husband is a Marine, isn't he?" Granddad dropped his bantering tone. "I'd love to meet him."

She gathered her tray of meds together and headed for the door. "I'll let him know."

Granddad turned to Becky after the nurse left. "What are you waiting for? Go get the diary!"

She retrieved it from its hiding place in the trunk then sat in the chair beside Granddad's bed and found the place where she'd left off.

The page she turned to was filled with a masterful drawing of soldiers engaged in many different activities. In one corner was a man who was deep in thought as he sketched on a board. In another corner was someone doing pull ups with sweat pouring down his face. Another part of the page held a group of men sitting around eating dinner looking as though someone had just told a good joke. Another sketch was of someone looking off into the distance thinking about something serious. Becky sat and stared at the drawings for a while. The details were impressive. It was almost as good as a photograph. If any of these men walked down the street she would recognize them in an instant.

"Would you please hold up that sketch so I can see it better?" Granddad asked.

Becky held it a couple feet from his face.

"Good ole Bill," Granddad said, as though talking to himself. "And Dave and Leroy from New York City. And there's Scott. He was the runt of us. That's him doing pull ups. He was always doing pull ups or pushups. He couldn't do even one when we first started and by the end of the war, thanks to not wanting any of us to be in better shape than him, he could do them with one arm."

He closed his eyes, remembering. Becky stayed quiet. She got the feeling that going through this diary was hard on him and wanted for him to deal with the memories at a pace he could handle.

His eyes opened and he smiled at her. "You aren't much of a chatter box, are you?"

"I try not to be."

"How about you start reading again," he said. "I got a good sleep last night so I oughta be able to stay awake longer today."

She turned the page and began to read aloud.

There is mass confusion. Everything we do is supposed to be hush-hush, but it seems no one knows for sure what's going to happen or what this big secret plan is all about. All we know is that we are going to be used to deceive the Nazis. When we talked in the bunks last night we discovered that all of us have different but specific skills.

Some of us are painters and sculptors. Some of us are radio guys and have the technical skills to work at radio stations. Some are professional actors. Then there's this one guy who made a living as a magician!

We've only been told the bare essentials. Somehow we are going to be using our odd mixture of skills to fool the enemy, but how we can pull that off I don't know. The Germans fly their planes over our troops and we do the same. Time will tell . . . time will tell.

CHAPTER
THIRTEEN

"I don't understand." Becky looked up from the book. "A magician? How could a magician help? All of you were soldiers, though, right? There's a lot of this I don't understand."

"Welcome to our world at that time," Granddad said. "There was a lot that we didn't understand either. It was what they began to call World War II, but we didn't have any history books to tell us what it was all about. The generals were kind of writing history as they went along. The chapter about us was brand new and had never been written before. The people in charge of us thought they had a good idea, but they were feeling their way along. Keep reading, though, and you'll start to figure out—like we did— what they had planned for us."

"Okay." Becky turned a page and began to read.

It has finally been made clear to us what our mission is. We are creating a stage, a play if you will, to deceive the Nazis. There are those who think the job we have been given is crazy, but I disagree. One of our first assignments is to use our skills to trick the Nazis and draw their fire so they don't shoot the real troops. Then, the real troops can come around, surprise the Nazis and attack at their weak locations.

I guess maybe it is a little crazy, but that's the plan and we're determined to make it work. If it doesn't, we might all end up speaking German and I've never been good with languages.

I've been assigned to work with the 603rd Camouflage Engineers. They are an amazing group. One of their assignments was camouflaging buildings in the USA along the coast so that if the Nazis send bombers to the U.S. they wouldn't see the important buildings like our aircraft plants.

I seem to have a talent for building camouflage around land vehicles and that is what they have me do. I can make a tank blend right in with a forest or make it look like nothing is there, just like you are looking at an empty field. So many other talented folks are here and we play to each other's strengths. We have the 244th Signal Company which employs radio counter intelligence tricks. There is the

3132nd Signal Service Company. They have been making recordings of the 'sounds of war.' These are everything from the sounds of hammers hitting nails to supposedly build bridges to tanks crossing rivers.

We've tested how far we could hear them blasting these sounds. We could hear these sounds from almost fifteen miles away and it sounded just like the real thing. They use some sort of wire to record on.

Then we have the 406th Engineer Combat Company. These are the guys who are trained to both fight and build. They're in charge of our security but do construction as well. All four units make up the 23rd Headquarters Special Troops.

Becky glanced up from the diary. "So, that's how you got started making camouflage clothing?"

"Yes." Granddad nodded. "I seemed to have a knack for making things blend in. When I came back from the war it was hard to get a job—there were so many soldiers coming back and entering the work force all at once—so I figured I might as well start my own business. It was a risk, but I knew I had to try. With the pay I saved up during the war it was just enough to obtain a few sewing machines and material."

"Was it hard?" Becky had never known anyone who

had started a business from scratch, let alone an artist who had done so.

"It seemed like I worked twenty-four hour days that first year. It was cheaper for me to do the work than to hire seamstresses. I had to give away a lot of clothing at first to convince hunters that I had the best. One man came in bragging that he had held out some corn and held still. He said that the deer walked up and ate the corn right out of his hand. It turned out that he worked for a hunting magazine and he wrote a story about my clothing factory. From that moment on, my designs started selling. Then some general saw the article. He came and bought a hunting outfit for himself and asked what else I could make. Before long I had a contract to sell camouflage to the U.S. Army. It felt good to use my skills to help protect those I had served with."

"Claire told me that you were a clerk for the Army and was stationed in London," Becky said. "Was she lying?"

"No," Granddad smiled. "I did some clerking type work in London for a couple months. I was stationed in London but not for the entire war. No one much cares to hear what a clerk does so I didn't have to answer many questions."

"Why didn't you ever tell your family the whole truth?" Becky asked.

"What we did was top secret for years. Then, I just . . .

I don't know. People expect a soldier to fight with bullets. I did fight—but with a paint brush."

"But why are you telling me instead of them?"

"You have to admit, it is a strange story. I had to go so long without telling it. I think I've been afraid they wouldn't believe me. Once we were allowed to talk about it, I was half-afraid Rusty and Claire might think I was getting more senile than I am. I guess I'm telling you about it now is because we are so much alike—and someone needs to know."

"Alike?" Becky glanced down at her young white arm lying next to his which was wrinkled and so much darker.

"Yes. Alike. You were born with an artist's heart. You have the talent to do something great. You just don't know it yet. I was a black artist in New York. No one paid me a bit of attention until that one person saw me for what I was and what I could do. Because someone trusted and believed in me, I helped save lives. Our unit is credited with saving about thirty-thousand fathers, brothers, sons, and husbands who grew old with loved ones, saw their grandkids grow up, helped humankind. They are not under tombstones in Europe or Missing in Action, and for that I smile."

CHAPTER
FOURTEEN

The next sketch in Granddad's book was of a line of men throwing up over the railing of a ship. Becky began to read.

So we have continued to train and learn and now I can't believe it, but it's May. We have worked with so many units and learned to impersonate so many different outfits that many of us have bloody fingertips from removing and attaching different shoulder patches. We've been joking that we should get purple hearts for our sewing injuries."

Becky glanced up from the page. "What's a purple heart?"

"It's a medal you receive for being injured in combat."

"Did you get one?" she asked.

Granddad looked away, deep in thought. Then he

shook his head. "Let's save that conversation for another day. For now, just read. It's been a long time since I heard these words."

So after working with inflatable rubber tanks, rubber artillery guns, fake radio transmissions, etc. we have set sail on the USS Henry Gibbons to Great Britain. A lot of us have never been on a ship, much less a ship going across the ocean. Many of us will be happy to make landfall. I have heard that when combat troops storm beaches from, boats it is usually not hard to get them off the boat because they are so sea sick. I now understand that feeling! We have all lost weight on this journey because of all the sea sickness we have endured. And yet, we have trained hard and are at the peak of our athletic ability. Most of us have never seen combat but we think we spend as much energy setting up fake fighting units as do the real units.

Becky looked at the next drawing. It was of soldiers sitting around small tables at what appeared to be an outdoor restaurant. Beneath the drawing Granddad's neat printing began again.

It has been a long few weeks. No one quite knows what to do with us. They say it will be soon. There is some buzz of a massive U.S. invasion into France. I'm scared but also want to "get in the fight." If others are going in harm's way it is my job to make it hard for the Nazis to get them! In the meantime we continue to work out and build our endurance. We know it will have to be nonstop work when we set up a fake unit because many will need to go up overnight. However, I can't complain about where we are. I actually have had time to go to Shakespeare plays and drink tea at cafés. In a lot of ways London is like New York and in other ways it is very different.

"This next drawing is scary, Granddad," Becky said.

Granddad partially sat up. "Which one is it?"

"There are men on a beach and it looks like they are wounded. Medics and nurses are everywhere."

He lay back against the pillows and sighed. "It looks scary because it was scary. Just keep reading."

Nothing can describe the horrors I've seen and yet I'm a week late. I was part of the first group from the 23rd that landed at Omaha Beach. It was D+7.

"D+7," Becky said. "I have no idea what that means."

"It had been seven days since the U.S. and their allies

had landed on the French beaches in Normandy," Granddad said. "There were terrible casualties, but keep reading."

"Okay," Becky said, "but I'm starting to wish I'd paid more attention during world history class."

We think the fighting is over on the beaches at that point. All the wounded have been waiting to be transported out to any hospital they could be shipped to and they are so pitiful. It's the first I've ever been remotely close to the real horrors of war. Up until that point, it has been something I've heard about or read about. Now it's real and I'm in the middle of it.

Tonight, as I was carrying some of our equipment up the beach, a medic screamed at me to come hold an IV bottle. I ran over and held the bottle as best I could without shaking while the medic continued to work over a horribly wounded solider. The soldier couldn't have been older than eighteen. I am just a few years older than him.

I have never felt so helpless and worthless as at that moment. I know nothing about treating wounds. After a bit the medic stopped and stood up.

"He's passed on," the medic said. Then he took the IV bottle from my hand and ran to the next wounded soldier.

I'm still in shock. I have never watched anyone die before. Here was somebody's brother, son, or husband.

There was nothing else I could do but grab my equipment and keep walking down the beach. I remember with shame the stupid Purple Heart jokes we had said about our sewing injuries.

Until that moment, I had been an artist who had been recruited to do a job. It was seeing the wounded that turned me into a soldier. I became deadly focused on using my talents to become the best at tricking the Nazis and drawing their fire away from the soldiers who were fighting this war.

To add to my grim determination, some artillery shells came from miles away from the Germans. I dove to the ground and prayed. Then, when I realized I was still alive, I got up and kept moving our equipment. Four men from the 23rd were wounded on that day. I was one of them.

Becky gasped. "You were wounded?"

"I was," Granddad said. "A shell exploded not too far away and a small piece sliced my left arm pretty good. But my injury was a mosquito bite compared to the wounded I saw. I was able to bandage it until our medic could properly tend to it. It barely slowed me down. I was so mad at the Nazis that I was able to bury the pain and keep going."

"So did you get a Purple Heart?" Becky asked.

"My captain put in for it but the paperwork was lost

somewhere. After seeing what a real wound looked like, I didn't feel like pursuing it."

Becky started to read again, but Granddad stopped her.

"Reliving that time is harder on me than I realized," Granddad said. "It was a terrible time. I'd like to rest now. We can do some more tomorrow when you come."

CHAPTER
FIFTEEN

The next morning, during her and Rusty's morning run, Becky stopped dead in her tracks and just stared. They were running through the downtown square in Kosciusko when the blank brick wall of Troyer drug store filled Becky's vision. Seeing that huge wall was like seeing a blank white canvas.

Rusty stopped alongside her, looked at what she was staring at and apparently read her mind.

"Are you wishing you could paint that wall?" he asked.

"Well, yes. It would make a great canvas, but I've learned my lesson. I'm not going to do anything that stupid again."

"Actually, I've been running you by this stupid wall for three weeks now waiting to see if you would notice," Rusty laughed. "Let's go in and talk to Mr. Troyer and see what he thinks about letting you decorate his building."

Becky was nervous. This was the first time she had

ever asked permission to draw on a building's wall, but she followed Rusty inside the store.

"Hi, Rusty. I haven't seen you in a while," Mr. Troyer said from behind the counter when they entered. "It's people like you who exercise to stay healthy who will run me out of business someday. How's your dad doing?"

"Oh, he still thinks he's twenty. Becky here has been visiting with him every day."

"Is that so?" Mr. Troyer said. "Tell him I'll stop by in a few days to visit with him even though he was in the Army."

"I don't understand," Becky said. "What's wrong with being in the Army?"

"I've always told him that he should have joined the Navy like me," Mr. Troyer said. "Here I am, ninety years old and still working."

"Hey, now, if you want to start telling Army jokes," Rusty said, "I've got a bunch of Navy ones saved up from Dad."

"Like what?" Mr. Troyer looked interested.

Rusty turned toward Becky. "Do you know what the Navy is good for?"

"No," she said.

"Nothing except using their boats to take the Army guys to the fight!"

"That joke is older than I am," Mr. Troyer groaned.

"Army guys can't come up with anything original. What he's not telling you is that if the Army guys had to transport themselves to the fight, they would end up at the South Pole!"

At that point he stuck out his hand to shake Becky's. "Army guys also don't have any manners. He's not introduced us yet. I'm Ralph Troyer, the owner and eye candy of Troyer Drug Store."

"I'm Becky." She shook his hand.

"Becky is from Chicago," Rusty said. "She decided she was tired of the city and came down to Mississippi to stay with us and get some clean air for a few months."

Becky was grateful that Rusty didn't embarrass her by saying her decision was court ordered.

"There's no state finer than Mississippi," Mr. Troyer said. "In fact, when I got off my ship for the last time in Mobile after the war ended, I kissed the ground and said I would never leave again."

"Becky has an idea she would like to ask you about," Rusty said.

"An idea?" Mr. Troyer gave his full attention to Becky. "I'm listening."

"Sir, people tell me I can draw and paint pretty good," Becky said, timidly. "I see your wall outside is completely blank. I was wondering . . . if I could come up with a good idea would you let me paint it?"

"Hmmm." Mr. Troyer stroked his chin. "I've actually thought about doing something like that. I used to have an advertisement painted there, but it faded long ago. I really don't want to have another advertisement. If you can come up with a good idea, I'll consider it."

"Thank you," Becky said. "I'll give it my best shot!"

"Come on, Becky," Rusty said. "It's 8 o'clock in the morning. Time for this Navy guy to get his morning nap."

Rusty gave a casual salute and went out the door as the old man yelled with pretend indignation, "I'll give y'all a head start!"

"Mr. Troyer is a great man," Rusty said as they continued their run. "He still tries to deliver medicine to those who can't come get it or have no family to help them. He saw some of the worst fighting ever. One ship he worked on, The Indianapolis, was sunk. He spent four days clinging to debris until he was rescued. He also lost a lot of good friends who were trapped on the boat as it went down. How he was able to keep his good sense of humor all this time is a testament to the kind of man he is."

Becky was excited to think about that big brick wall to draw on and told Granddad about it as soon as Claire dropped her off. Instead of spending the two hours visit reading to him out of the diary, they spent their time discussing different ideas to paint on Mr. Troyer's wall. They considered everything from flowers to portraits of presidents. Then Becky came up with an idea that was so exciting, she could hardly sit still while she described it to Granddad. When she finished telling him about it, he smiled.

"Get out the sketching paper," he said. "We have work to do."

CHAPTER
SIXTEEN

It was Saturday night and Claire wanted Becky to go to church in the morning.

"I got you a new dress to wear," Claire said. "It's hanging in your closet."

Becky didn't know what to say. Not only had she never been inside a "real" church building, she had never in her life worn a dress. She walked upstairs, battling the fear that it might be something frilly. She had never thought of herself as a girly-girl.

She needn't have worried. Claire had good taste. Hanging in her closet was a simple blue dress made of a light flower pattern. She also noticed some new flats sitting there as well.

The next morning after she'd showered, she put on the church outfit and came down the stairs feeling a little bit self-conscious.

Claire and Rusty were sitting at the breakfast table when she came down. Becky cleared her throat and Rusty glanced up. The look he gave her seemed disapproving at first, and her heart fell. She'd hoped she looked nice in the pretty dress.

Then, he grinned mischievously. "Well, Claire," he said. "If some boys come knocking on our door because of how pretty she is, they are going to have to deal with me! I've got a shovel, a gun, and an alibi that I'm sure Dad will back me up on. You do realize you aren't allowed to date until you are twenty-five?"

"Girl, you look wonderful." Claire slapped Rusty on the arm. "Let's get you some breakfast. Then off to church we go."

"Is there something special about today?" Becky asked. "I've been here three weeks and this is the first time you've mentioned going to church."

"We wanted you settle in first and not shove you into anything," Claire said, "but I think you're going to enjoy it."

"We have a great youth program but if you're too nervous you can just sit with us until you are comfortable," Rusty said as he drove them to church.

"I'd rather sit with you," she said quickly. Church? This was way outside her comfort zone.

Once they were inside, however, two girls near her

age walked up and introduced themselves as Emma and Makenzie. They helped steer her to teen Bible class before she could even look around. Becky had never experienced such genuinely friendly kids. Her other friends were always wanting something from her or trying to take something away from her.

The teacher was funny and kept her attention. She had never touched a Bible before or had even heard any Bible stories. The kids with her were full of energy but not rude. Class seemed to pass quickly, and then she went into the auditorium. She felt a little guilty for not sitting with Claire and Rusty, but her new friends insisted that she sit with them towards the front. When she glanced at Claire to see if it was okay, Claire just smiled and nodded her head as if saying just go on and enjoy yourself.

The music was very different from anything she'd ever heard. There were no instruments, just pure voices. She did not know any of the songs, so she just kind of moved her lips and listened. The preacher used an illustration of a very long rope and said that this rope represented eternity and how only the first inch represented our life on earth.

Before she knew it church was over. She traded phone numbers with her new friends and they said they would call her later to do something in the week. She wondered if they were actually serious. She loved Granddad, Claire and

Rusty, but it would be nice to have some friends her own age while she was here.

CHAPTER
SEVENTEEN

Becky awoke every morning feeling increasingly more different than she had before she came to Kosciusko. There was so much to do and all of it was enjoyable, but spending time with Granddad was just about the most fascinating thing she'd ever done. Reading that diary to him and looking at his drawings was like stepping into a different world.

Today, the sketch in the diary was of a large man blowing a bubble from chewing gum.

"This is an odd picture," she said. "What's it about?"

"Oh, that is one of my favorite stories," Granddad said. "It shows how creative we had to get at solving problems. You're going to enjoy this story. I'm looking forward to hearing you read it to me."

Last night we slowly switched places with an artillery group. They would move out a real artillery piece and then we would replace it would an inflatable look-alike. It sounds easy, but it was a lot of work to time it just right. Plus, we had to do it in the dark and had to be so careful.

We got all the rubber pieces inflated and thought we'd accomplished our mission, but then the sun began to rise. To our horror, two of our fake pieces had leaks in the barrel and the barrel was drooping. Nothing would tip off the Germans faster than seeing drooping guns. Metal does not droop. Some of the men started shouting for someone to do something. We ran for the repair kits but for some reason no one could find the jeep that had them. It took me and a captain a full ten minutes to find the jeep, which had been parked further away and we came driving back.

The sun was above the horizon by the time we got back and turned off the jeep, we could hear the engine of a German reconnaissance plane. Those planes would always fly at first light to try and get pictures.

We hurried to the two inflatables that were damaged and to our surprise; the gun barrels were straight again. We turned to Frank O'Riley who was the one tending them and asked how he'd fixed them when we had all the repair kits.

He just smiled and said, "You guys owe me a new pack of bubble gum."

Frank had been able to plug the holes with bubble gum

and it worked perfectly until we could permanently fix the holes.

A few weeks later a major was visiting our site. We were eating and he yelled out, "Where is Frank O'Riley?"

Frank nervously raised his hand and said, "I'm here, sir."

The major threw him a package the size of a cigar box and said, "Here is a box of gum to replace the pack you used up the other day. Smart thinking soldier. I'm certain you saved some of my guys."

Everyone laughed while Frank tucked the box under his arm and gave a salute.

Granddad was smiling when she looked up from finishing the story. "From that day on we called him Bubble Gum O'Riley. What was even more amazing is that the box of gum the major gave him saved us a few months later when it was used for the same thing!"

Claire came earlier than usual to pick her up and she seemed worried. "We're down two people at the factory today and we have a large order to get together. Would you mind if I took Becky a little early, Dad? We could really use her help."

"Who is the order for?" he asked.

"It's a special order for a unit of U.S. soldiers in Iraq.

Two of our seamstresses are out on maternity leave and we're falling behind."

"You two girls get on out of here," he said, "and don't come back until those orders are filled. You know how I feel about supporting our troops."

"I do," Claire said.

Becky had never hugged Granddad before, but after what she'd learned in his diary, she felt like she had grown closer to him than anyone she'd ever known. Without asking permission, she leaned over the bed and gave him a gentle hug.

"Thank you," she whispered. "For everything."

He didn't respond with words, but he patted her back as she embraced him. She'd never had a grandfather before, but if she could have picked one, this old man is the person she would have chosen for herself.

"Remember," he said as Claire and she went out the door, "doing a good job means you're saving lives."

"I'll remember," Becky said.

A few minutes later, she was inside the small factory and Claire was showing her what to do. Working there was interesting and rewarding. Best of all, the other workers as well as Rusty and Claire did not treat her like some stupid street kid. They gave her real responsibilities and acted like they assumed she could accomplish them.

Today, she was working in the order fulfillment department. She was handed a big list of product numbers that described type of clothing, size, pant or shirt. At first it was a little hard to understand, but slowly the system came together for her.

There were hundreds of items. She picked out everything that had been ordered and laid everything out on the tables. Then the order fulfillment supervisor double checked everything. To her frustration she had made a few small mistakes.

"You did great for your first time!" The supervisor's name was Milly and she was about the age Becky's mother might have been.

"But I wanted it to be perfect." Becky was frustrated with herself. "I can't make any mistakes or it might affect our troops."

"It's my job to catch the mistakes," Milly said. "It's your job to simply do your best. It took me a full week to figure out this system. You've already gotten the hang of it. I think you're doing pretty good—especially for a kid."

Becky felt better after that. She helped Milly and the others pack up everything, put it on a pallet and watched as it was loaded on the truck. Then the truck drove away. It made her feel good to know that in a few weeks some soldier would be wearing the stuff she'd helped pack.

It was also fun eating lunch with the workers. Claire ran home and made her a basic bologna sandwich and chips to eat, but she looked across the table at Milly and saw her eating something that looked kind of like fried chicken, except it wasn't.

"What is that?" she asked, pointing at Milly's lunch. "Fried chicken?"

Christine burst out laughing, "It's fried catfish. You've never had fried catfish before?"

"Not really."

"Where are you from, girl?" Milly asked.

"Chicago."

"What kind of food do they eat in Chicago?"

"Hot dogs, hamburgers, pizza mainly—when I could get them."

Milly looked at her closely. "What do you mean, 'when you could get them?'"

Becky wondered how much to reveal. She usually told people as little as possible about herself because it was just safer that way. The thing was, she liked Milly and felt safe with the middle-aged woman. "Sometimes my foster parents could be kind of stingy when it came to food."

Milly nodded her head as though she understood perfectly. She didn't ask any follow-up questions, but she did put a large piece of her fried catfish on Becky's paper plate.

"It's not as good as fresh-cooked, but you'll get the idea."

Becky took a bite, chewed and the "Wow!" she involuntarily uttered was more heartfelt than she'd intended.

Milly smiled, "Oh, we are going to have to take you for your first fresh fried cat fish dinner after work sometime this week. Aren't we people?"

The rest of the workers sitting at the table nodded and chimed in by suggesting favorite catfish restaurants.

"Let's get back to work," Milly crumbled up the sack she'd brought her lunch in. "If we work hard we could have the rest of the special orders filled by tomorrow afternoon— especially with Becky here helping."

Becky realized at that moment that she was happier than she could remember being in a long, long time. She was starting to like Mississippi a whole lot. The only sadness was knowing she'd have to go back to Chicago at the end of the summer.

CHAPTER
EIGHTEEN

The orders had been filled on time and Claire and Rusty were delighted. Today she was back reading to Granddad. This morning there was another sketch to study. It was four men lifting a tank. Off in the distance was another solider talking to a farmer as though questioning him about something.

"There was no handbook for what we were doing," Granddad explained. "When we got to France, our biggest fear was that a German spy would tell his command that the United States had a fake army. We worried even that a civilian might find out and accidentally let someone know who was a German sympathizer.

One day we were setting up our equipment and testing each inflatable. One kind of inflatable we had was a tank. Well, somehow this French farmer had gotten through our security looking for a few of his animals that had gotten loose. One of our MP's ran over to him."

"MP?" Becky asked.

"I'm sorry," Granddad said. "That stands for Military Police."

"Okay. Go on."

"Once the MP got to him, the Frenchman saw the tank being lifted by four soldiers in the distance and his mouth was hanging open. The MP could speak French and told the farmer, "Americans are very strong!""

"What happened then?" Becky was entranced. This was so much better than history class!

Granddad laughed at the memory. "The farmer's eyes bugged out and then he turned and walked away as quickly as he could. We laughed later about the possibility of a German spy finding out that American soldiers could lift and move tanks!"

"I'll never forget the look on that farmer's face." Granddad was laughing so hard, tears ran down his cheeks. "I guess you had to be there."

The story was funny, but it was watching Granddad laugh so hard that made Becky start to giggle. Just then Rusty walked in the room and looked from Becky to Granddad and back again.

"What's so funny?" Rusty asked.

"Oh, Granddad and I were discussing an old story and his laughter is contagious."

Rusty didn't laugh. Instead he looked at Becky with respect and gratitude.

"I've not heard Dad laugh like that in months. It's such a blessing to have you here with us."

The comment nearly took Becky's breath away. No one had ever called her a blessing before. She had been called street trash, hooligan, loser, etc. but never had she been told that she was a blessing to someone. She had no idea how to take the compliment gracefully, but it surely did feel good and seemed to fill a hole inside of her that had been empty a long time.

"Could she stay a while longer, son?" Granddad said. "It feels like we just got started. After she goes home, the day seems to get awfully long."

"If you're sure talking with her is not wearing you out," Rusty said.

"I'm sure."

"Then I'll go to the hardware store and pick up some things I need. I'll be back in an hour."

"Thank you, son."

As soon as Rusty left the room, Granddad pointed at the diary which Rusty had not seen because Becky was seated on the other side of the bed.

"Read," he said. "He'll be back soon and he's a nosy one, that boy is."

"But you're going to tell him, right?" Becky didn't feel entirely comfortable keeping the diary secret from Claire and Rusty.

"I am," Granddad said, "but not quite yet."

Becky had no idea what the next drawing meant. There were men standing there with artillery pieces and it appeared that there was a small explosion at their feet.

This past mission was really interesting. One member of our group had an idea we thought to be brilliant and it was. We had set up dummy artillery pieces about a mile in front of the real guns. Just when it got dark, the real guns opened up. What we did was set up the dummy guns with small explosives on the ground. When the big guns would go off, we would set off the small explosive. It was just enough to make a bang and flash.

What that did was confuse the enemy and they thought the artillery was a mile closer to them than it actually was. We knew their ammo was running low and that they only fired when they were sure of a target. Last night they fired their own artillery at us all night long. How none of us were hurt is a miracle. However, a few inflatables were filled with shrapnel holes and we quickly disposed of them so they could not be found.

The night was not perfect. A lot of times we could not time it right, so the real guns going off might not match the flash/bang we were doing for them. We've worked on the technical way to fix, this but my guess is there were some very confused Germans. We also have found out that they are running low on food. Perhaps, they are so hungry they didn't notice the delay and double sounds.

CHAPTER
NINETEEN

Becky had worked late into the night finishing the sketch of the drawing she was thinking of painting on the drugstore wall. She showed it to Granddad first. He made a few suggestions, which she implemented. Then she showed it to Rusty and he loved it. So off to the Troyer's drugstore they went.

As they walked in, they heard Mr. Troyer joking but also being serious with one of his older customers about the customer not taking her blood pressure medicine like she should.

"Mrs. Prescott, you can do this the easy way or the hard way," Mr. Troyer said. "Take your medicine like your doctor says, or I'll call the local vet and make him blow the pills down your throat like he has to do for horses!"

Mrs. Prescott laughed and put her hands up in a

defensive gesture. "Okay, you don't have to call the vet! I'll be good."

"Hey, Becky," Mr. Troyer said as they walked up to the counter. "Did Rusty ever tell you about his first job in the Army?"

"No, Mr. Troyer, he never did. Maybe you could tell me that story." Becky knew this was a set up, so she played along. Rusty just rolled his eyes.

"Rusty was on guard duty," Mr. Troyer leaned over the pharmacy counter. "His orders were clear. No vehicle was to enter his gate unless it had a special pass sticker on the windshield. A nice big Army car comes up with a four star general sitting in the back. Rusty says 'Halt! Who goes there?'"

"That never happened," Rusty said.

Mr. Troyer continued with his story as though Rusty wasn't there.

"Well, the driver says to Rusty, 'I'm transporting General Young.' and General Young ignores Rusty and tells the driver to drive on because he has an important meeting. Rusty says, 'Stop! You can't come through. I have orders to shoot if anyone tries driving in without a special sticker.' General Young says again, 'Drive on!'

"So, what does Rusty do? He walks up to the rear

window and says, 'General Young, I'm new at this. Who am I supposed to shoot? You or the driver?"

Mr. Troyer let out a belly laugh and Becky couldn't help but giggle.

"I didn't do that," Rusty said again. "But it's a great story. Have I told you about the one and only time Mr. Troyer was allowed to captain a ship off of the coast of Canada?"

Becky shook her head. "Nope, haven't heard that one."

"Well, he was sailing his ship up to Alaska from Los Angeles," Rusty said. "He noticed a light up ahead and he radioed, 'Please divert your course 15 degrees to the west to avoid a collision.'"

"Oh, I've heard this one," Mr. Troyer said. "You'll like this one, Becky. Go ahead, Rusty."

"The person at the light responded, 'Recommend you divert YOUR course 15 degrees to the west to avoid a collision.' So, Mr. Troyer gets right back on the radio. He's always been stubborn. He gets all huffy and radios back, 'This is Captain Troyer of a U.S. Navy Ship. I repeat, divert YOUR course!'"

"What happened then?" Becky couldn't wait to hear the punchline.

"Well the radio from the light responds again, 'Captain Troyer! I say again, divert YOUR course!' By now Mr. Troyer has had enough, so he yells through the radio, 'This is the Aircraft carrier USS Enterprise. We are one of the largest ships in the United States Navy Fleet. I have armed combat aircraft, four destroyers, four cruisers, and numerous other ships. I demand you change YOUR course or I will engage counter measures to ensure the safety of this ship!' Then, Mr. Troyer put down the radio. He was feeling all smug, knowing whoever was up ahead will finally be intimidated by his might."

"Were they?" Becky asked.

"The radio crackled again and the person at the microphone said, 'Captain Troyer, this is the lighthouse. The choice is yours.'"

Mr. Troyer cackled and smacked his knee in appreciation of the joke while Becky and Rusty shared a laugh. Then he said, "Rusty tells me that you have a drawing you wanted to show me. Is that true?"

"I hope you like it." Becky pulled out her sketch and handed it to him. "I worked really hard on it. Granddad helped."

They were all silent as Mr. Troyer studied the sketch. Becky didn't realize she was holding her breath until the old man glanced up at her and smiled.

"I love it!" Mr. Troyer exclaimed. "When can you start?"

CHAPTER
TWENTY

Becky was beginning to wonder if she could possibly get everything finished before she had to go back to Chicago at the end of the summer. There was Mr. Troyer's mural, and the time she spent reading and discussing Granddad's diary with him was precious to her. Unfortunately, today she couldn't go see him. He had a doctor's appointment in another city, and both Rusty and Claire were going to take him. Claire told her that it might take several hours before they were back.

They assigned her to a different section of the factory today while they were gone. That's how Becky ended up working in the computer design department of the plant. She knew how to use a computer, of course. Basic stuff every kid her age picked up, but when she met an intern, James, who was working there from the local college—she realized there was a whole world of computer design she'd never realized existed.

James was about ten years older than her and very serious about doing a good job. He told her that he was the first in his family to attend college and wanted to do well.

James took the time to show her some of the programs he used in creating clothing styles. She thought it might be like fashion designing, but the clothing he was working on had little to do with fashion and everything to do with safety, comfort, and of course—blending into the environment. It intrigued her where the company put hidden pockets and reinforced elbow material in case the soldiers had to crawl. Many of the designs used Velcro instead of buttons in some instances, but not always. James explained that the sound that Velcro made could be a problem in some situations. Buttons were clumsy but they were silent. Velcro was fast, but made a telltale sound when it was ripped open.

"There's a department of the military that is working on a top secret project trying to make "silent" Velcro," James told her. "They sent us some prototypes for us to experiment within a few of our designs but so far the perfect Velcro has not yet been created."

This fascinated Becky. She eagerly asked so many questions that James politely handed her off to Debbie, who was also in the design department, so he could get some more work done. Debbie kept Becky busy printing off proposed designs and taking them around to various departments in the plant, so other workers could look at the designs and make notes if they had any feedback. Then, Debbie fed the information to James who would sometimes make changes in the computer program he was working with.

Becky had no idea how much science was involved in making clothing and designing camo, but as she looked at the designs, she could see the patterns and shapes and realized that it was all just another form of art.

All this, she thought, from Granddad's work in The Ghost Army, the "army" that was visible but didn't really exist.

It was all amazing to her. She was waking every morning without the sense of dread that had once been her constant companion. In fact, nearly every day was filled with joy and eager anticipation. There simply were not enough hours in the day. Even some of the kids at church had called and invited her to go out with them. She didn't feel like she fit in all that well yet, but she liked being with kids who got a kick out of doing everyday stuff like going to movies and out for ice cream.

CHAPTER
TWENTY-ONE

Becky was especially looking forward to seeing Granddad the next day after his doctor appointment had kept them apart.

He seemed alert and eager to see her as well.

"You're going to like this one," he said, handing her the diary opened to a drawing she had not yet seen.

It was a group of guys looking drunk around a table and someone in a German uniform with huge ears trying to listen in.

Becky could hardly wait to start in.

Not only do we have world class artists in our unit, we have some great actors among us as well. We know the Nazis have spies everywhere. I often wonder why people spy for them. Maybe it is money, or their families are threatened, or, in some cases, they have swallowed the Nazi propaganda whole.

One of our favorite means to confuse and fool the Nazis has nothing to do with paint and camouflage and everything to do with acting and verbal deception. Some of our people go into the French towns and drink coffee or go to the bars. A lot of them don't really drink when they go in, but, goodness, they can act drunk!

When they are acting drunk, they start spouting off "secrets" that people are listening in on. Plus, they put on different unit patches. Our best "actors" pretend to be drunk and from another unit. They start talking about how many soldiers they have, and how many tanks, and where they are going next, etc.

When in truth, the unit we were pretending to be in is on the move miles away coming at the Germans from another direction. Some of the spies are obvious. Most are not and some of the times, our actors knew there were no spies around but still played the parts.

This is one of the hardest things our unit does and I have a lot of respect for those who use their acting abilities to spread wrong information. One of the hardest things they do is pretend to be people that they are not. Since most of the Army does not know about the Ghost Army, this becomes a problem when their rules apply to something we're trying to do—and they have no idea who we are.

For example, impersonating an officer will get any soldier into big trouble, but in order to fool the Nazis we sometimes grab one of our best actors and throw a general's stars on him. Then, he'll walk around town and talk, act, and strut like people would expect a general to do. Sometimes, other U.S. units will be passing through and wonder who this general is. He might be pretending to be a known general or an unknown general. Again, this is just to confuse the spies.

Unfortunately, our own soldiers sometimes run across one of our unit's actors who is trying to give out wrong information—which confuses them greatly--but we still have to keep our cover. If one of them is captured and they know the truth about us, they could disclose it to the Germans and totally give away what we are doing.

One close call we had recently is while we were pretending to be a particular tank unit. On the outskirts of our security perimeter, a soldier walked up and said he wanted to see his brother who was in the unit. He just happened to be passing through and thought he would visit. Of course, we knew his brother was about twenty miles away with the real unit. Our guard tried to stall, telling him that his brother wasn't part of the unit and that he'd never heard of him.

The soldier wouldn't take "no" for an answer. He kept insisting that he knew his brother was attached to this particular unit, and he just wanted to stop by and check on him. Finally, our guard "admitted" he was new to the unit and didn't know everyone. Enough time had been wasted by then that the soldier who was trying to make a short visit threw up his hands and had to drive on to meet up with the rest of his group. Unfortunately we had to play this ruse more than once. We don't like lying to our own guys, but for their own safety, we think we have to.

The next page revealed a picture of a tank, part of it visible under some cover.

The art of camouflage is a science. If we do it too well, the Germans simply won't see us at all. If we do it too badly, they will know something is wrong. So, we actually have a formula on how many things we hide perfectly, and how many others we make look like we really tried to hide things but made a couple major mistakes.

That method seems to work the best when they keep flying over to figure out what the strength of our force is. It is a wonder our military has not had more losses by now.

We have been called to do camouflage audits of other units. We, of course, do not tell officially where we are from, but we go and visit.

One thing some of us found amazing was how poorly the General's headquarters are hidden. By the time we are done with our audits, the units we visit are usually very grateful. We have even learned how many fires we should light to look like a real unit and how to hang laundry to make it look like a much larger force ready to attack. If lives were not in danger what we do could be fun—but lives are in danger and we are always aware that what we are doing is not play. We take it deadly serious.

CHAPTER
TWENTY-TWO

One of Becky's new friends from church gave her a call. It turned out that the teens were getting together on Friday night at one of the church elder's house for swimming, food, and Bible study. That didn't sound like all that much fun to her. Being invited to an "elder's" house had an intimidating feel to it.

Rusty drove her to the teen get-together and walked her into the house. Claire had given her a bag of chips to take with her and as Becky went inside, she laid the bag on the table. She was very worried that she wouldn't fit in and that she was dressed all wrong. Claire had told her to wear a t-shirt and shorts with a bathing suit underneath. It turned out that everyone was pretty much dressed the same way. After Rusty left and some of Becky's new girlfriends took her out to the swimming pool, she saw boys were being loud jumping off the diving board while the girls, for the most part, hung out in the shallow end and talked.

There were black kids, Hispanic kids, and white kids. Just like Chicago except they were all getting along and having fun. As Becky chatted with the other girls, she became more relaxed.

Just then above her someone yelled "Cannonball". She looked up and saw a gray haired man jump from his 2nd story porch, landing in the deep end doing a huge splash. The boys yelled and fist bumped approval of the older man when he surfaced.

"Who is that?" Becky asked.

"That's Bob," Emma said. "He's one of the elders at our church."

Becky smiled and shook her head. This was not exactly what she'd expected an elder to be like. After a bit, Bob's wife came out with a big tray of hot dogs and the kids dug in.

For Becky, this was a treasured moment. No gangs, no one trying to hurt each other—as long as she didn't count one of the boys chasing another boy and trying to shove a hotdog with lots of ketchup into his face.

Later on, after everyone had eaten all they wanted and worn themselves out swimming and having fun, Bob held a small devotional. They sang some songs she didn't know.

The songs were different than the music she usually listened to on the radio.

Then Bob talked to them about someone from the Bible he called the Prodigal Son. As she listened, Becky realized that she was starting to feel a lot like that lost son. She had been lost for a very long time, but it felt like she was being found again. Maybe not by her biological father—whoever he was—but by something even better. People who genuinely cared about her.

Soon it started to get dark. She thought things were winding down, but then someone yelled, "Flashlight tag!"

In the woods behind Bob's house, she learned the fine art of flashlight tag. For the next hour she ran with Emma. Again the sounds were so pleasant. She heard giggling, laughing, and a bit of good natured trash talking in the dark as the kids ran around trying to tag each other.

Finally, head lights starting showing up at the house as the parents began showing up to get their kids. Rusty pulled up and stood outside the car, smiling, while she said good-bye to her new friends.

"You enjoy yourself?" he asked as he held the door open for her.

She climbed into the front seat and waved at some of the other kids as they drove away.

"It was the best time I've ever had," she said. "My

stomach hurts from laughing so much. No body tried to hurt anybody and I didn't have to be afraid even once."

"That's good to hear, sweetie," he said.

The swimming and running around in the woods had worn her out, so she leaned her head back against the seat and closed her eyes.

She did not see the grim set to Rusty's mouth as he drove or the unshed tears that he wiped from his eyes.

CHAPTER
TWENTY-THREE

Becky walked into Granddad's room and gave him a hug. This had become customary over the weeks they'd spent together.

"Granddad," she said. "Could I ask a very personal question that I have no business asking?"

"I've already trusted you with my most closely guarded secrets. You can ask me anything."

Becky took a deep breath, "Why don't Rusty and Claire have any children of their own?"

"I wondered when you would ask that." Granddad smiled sadly. "They lost a little girl to a terrible disease. She was only three. I won't go into every detail. It's too heartbreaking, but we were all devastated when she died."

"I'm so sorry," Becky said.

"It was a tough time but we got through it," Granddad

said. "Claire was never able to have children again. It's been hard on her."

"But the first day I came in here, you asked me if I was one of your grandchildren. Were you just making a joke?"

"It was a joke, but I do have other grandchildren and even three great-grandchildren. My other son lives in Oregon with his wife. They have six kids who are all grown up now. They used to bring the kids and visit each Christmas. Rusty and Claire would spoil those children something terrible. Way too many presents. Claire would shop for weeks."

"Why didn't Claire and Rusty just adopt?" Becky asked.

"I never asked them, but I think they were afraid to risk loving another child and maybe losing it, too."

"Rusty and Claire treat me better than anyone ever has," Becky said. "I'm sorry they've been through such a hard time."

"Best you don't bring it up," Granddad said. "Old wounds are sometimes better left alone. Now . . . the diary?"

The sketch Becky saw in Granddad's diary was of men with earphones sitting around a radio. One of them was touching some sort of small switch. In another picture there was a truck with a huge loud speaker on it.

Granddad had begun to sleep a lot more since his trip to the doctor and seemed less inclined to talk, so she started reading immediately, hoping to get a good start before he nodded off.

We don't always rely on our inflatables and visible tricks and actors. An equally important art of deception is sound and communication. I'll admit that I get a bit lost hearing the ones who deal with the communication systems talk about what they do—all of it is so technical. One thing I have learned is that the way a telegraph communicator types out his messages is as unique as a finger print even though they use the same code language. When I listen, all I hear is dot-dot-dot, dash-dash-dash, but experienced operators are so good they know who is on the other end by their style. Doesn't matter if they identify themselves or not. The Germans know this, too. So we go one step further with this.

Our guys study the telegraph communicators from each of the divisions. They do the same thing with the Germans. They can tell who is at the key just by their style. Sometimes being able to mimic another operator's style perfectly is important to pulling off a misdirection or deception.

We were given a mission of just trying to fool the Nazis with nothing more than sound and radio. For the entire day before, we typed out orders of movements of tanks to a certain location. Then that night we drove trucks with huge speakers on them while playing sounds of tanks moving into position. Just sounds of armored tanks moving into position—nothing else. This went on for all night. The goal was to confuse the enemy into thinking an armored division was moving into a false location when in fact the real tank division was moving into an entirely different location.

The "brass" wanted to make sure the Germans kept their defenses in place instead of moving them. What we did must have worked, because the next morning when first light started showing, we could see that the Nazis had in fact not moved.

I wish I could have seen their faces as they looked through their binoculars trying to see the positions into which they'd heard all those tanks move the night before, only to see nothing but open fields and trees.

They shot off some artillery to see if they could spook anyone out who might be hiding but of course they blasted holes in the ground. I hoped that the farmer's field needed to be plowed anyways!

Of course, we usually never know if what we are doing is actually fooling the Germans or not. If there is one thing we never allow ourselves to do is underestimate the enemy's intelligence. Still, we think we are fooling them because fire does come in at us from time to time. However today we obtained confirmation that we were not working in vain.

We were given a brief from Army Intelligence that they had recently captured some Germans soldiers. During their interrogation they learned that the Germans had been tracking this "Phantom Army" but could never find it. A lot of resources of reconnaissance planes and intelligence officers had been assigned to track down this "Phantom Army" but they were always one step behind.

Of course, they had found us, but they did not realize that we were the phantom army and what they thought was a real combat division was actually us! We were over-joyed to hear our efforts and resources were working. Even if we confused the Germans for just a few hours it meant lives of U.S. soldiers were being saved. After hearing this, we had even more enthusiasm for our work. As we became more skilled, we doubled our effort.

Becky could tell that Granddad was sound asleep now. When he was asleep, his mouth tended to hang open a little. When he was just resting his eyes, that didn't happen. She didn't want to quit reading, but it wasn't as much fun when Granddad wasn't alert and talking with her about the things she read. She closed the diary and waited for him to wake up. Sometimes he did if she stopped reading for a bit—as though the sound of her voice comforted him and when she stopped, he automatically woke up.

Today, he didn't wake up. He seemed to be sleeping very soundly. Too soundly. She longed for him to awaken and talk to her again. Maybe even tease her a little. She missed him.

At church there was always a lot of talk about prayer. This wasn't something she was used to, but as she sat beside Granddad's bed, the need to talk to someone bigger than her felt nearly overwhelming. She folded her arms on Granddad's bed, laid her head on them, and closed her eyes. Her prayer was halting, but it was real. She asked for God to make Granddad better, to make him not sleep as much, to not take him away from her.

She didn't realize he could hear her until she felt Granddad's hand gently stroking her head.

"It's okay, Becky," Granddad said. "I'm just tired from the doctor's visit the other day. I won't be leaving you yet. I have too much to live for, especially now that you're here."

When she lifted her head, she realized her cheeks were wet and she hadn't even realized that she'd been crying. It had been years since she'd cried over anything, or anyone. Granddad had grown to mean so much to her that she'd begun to wonder how she could bear to leave him and Rusty and Claire and go back to Chicago. It was going to break her heart, but she knew it was inevitable. Suddenly, the tears began to flow even faster, and there was nothing she could do to stop them.

CHAPTER
TWENTY-FOUR

The youth group from church was heading to Jackson, the capital of Mississippi. They were going to visit with an inner city church and help distribute basic supplies to the street people. She didn't want to miss an entire day with Granddad and his Ghost Army diary, but Rusty and Claire insisted she go.

So here she was, on a church bus, on her way to help street people. She almost laughed at the irony. Wasn't she technically homeless? Yes, she had a roof over her head with Rusty and Claire but what about this fall? What then?

Some of the kids sang to tunes on the radio. Others played on their phones, and others just talked with each other. She joined the discussion of the newest boy band heart throb, nail polish, where they thought they would go to college, and being a "Bulldog fan," but Becky kept thinking about how lucky these kids were to have nothing more important to worry about than the color of their nail polish.

Still, once they arrived in the inner-city the day went by faster than she thought. She saw herself in so many of the kids that came through the food line. She spent time talking with the street kids while walking around refilling drinks and getting them more food. She had a connection with them that the others could not.

She knew about their lives and their pain. She knew about their hunger and their hopelessness.

On the way home, the other kids were subdued. Conversations about nail polish and boy bands were non-existent. Instead, there seemed to be a lot of deep thought going on.

Mackenzie, one of the girls she'd come to know, came and sat down behind Emma and her.

"You seemed to really connect with the people we helped today," Mackenzie said. "What's up with that?"

Becky hesitated. Did she really want these other kids to know her story?

"It's okay." Emma put her hand over hers and said, "We care about you. Please trust us."

Becky's story came pouring out in such a torrent that even she was shocked. She explained about being abandoned, talked about the countless couches and floors she had slept on, and told them the real reason she was in Mississippi. When she finally stopped, she waited for judging eyes and faces.

Instead, Emma said, "Well, honey, if you ever need another couch to crash on come on to my house!"

"Or mine," Mackenzie said. "Mom and Dad are used to having lots of kids around. I was a foster kid myself until they took me in and then adopted me. I have four siblings at my house and not one of us is blood related."

Becky was astonished. Not only were Emma and Mackenzie not making fun of her, they seemed to understand, at least at some level. The fact that they had become true friends gave her a feeling of warmth in her heart that she'd seldom experienced.

That evening when she got home, she asked Rusty and Claire if maybe she could go visit Granddad since she'd not gotten to see him at her regular time that day. Rusty and Claire glanced at each other, but she couldn't read their expressions. Were they worried that she'd tire the old man out?

"I'll be careful," she promised. "If he starts getting tired, I'll stop reading and call you. I promise."

"It isn't that," Rusty said. "It's just that the nurse said he'd been asking for you all day. She said he seemed to be worried that you'd gone back to Chicago without telling him. I went over a little while ago and reassured him that you were fine, but you'd taken a trip with the youth group and would come in to see him tomorrow. I wasn't going to ask, but if you wouldn't mind going over tonight it would really please him . . . and us."

"I'm ready," she turned to go out the door.

"Don't you want to rest up from your trip and eat a bite?" Claire asked.

"No," Becky answered. "I just want to see Granddad. He usually saves a few crackers or cookies from his lunch for me anyway. It'll make him happy if I'm actually hungry for them when I get there."

When they arrived, Rusty went in with her to check on his father. Granddad was dozing in front of the TV which was turned to "The Price Is Right." He woke up immediately when he heard their voices.

"Turn that thing off!" he commanded. "Where have you been, Becky?"

"I told you, Dad," Rusty said. "She went with the church youth group to work in a soup kitchen feeding the homeless."

Granddad asked for his glasses, which she handed him. Then he looked deep into her eyes. "Was that hard on you? Are you all right?"

"It was very hard," she admitted, "but I kept thinking

about my nice room at Rusty and Claire's and how good they've been to me and yes, I'm okay." She gave the old man a hug. "I'm especially okay now that I'm here."

Granddad patted her back and even though her face was buried in his chest, she could almost feel him smiling.

"Been having trouble sleeping," Granddad said. "It'll help having this girl here reading to me, son. I appreciate you bringing her over."

"I'll go check in at the factory," Rusty said. "We've had to put on an extra shift until we get that special order of desert uniforms finished. I'll be back in an hour. Anything you need me to pick up for you?"

"Blue Bell chocolate chip mint ice cream," Granddad said. "I've been lying here thinking about how much your mother loved Blue Bell chocolate chip mint ice cream. Thought about it so long, I've started craving it myself."

"I can't guarantee they'll have any, but I'll stop at the store on my way back," Rusty said with a wave.

"Saved some Nutter Butters from dinner for you," Granddad said after Rusty had gone. "I had a feeling you might come to visit after you got home. Are you hungry?"

"I'm starved," Becky said, "and Nutter Butters are my favorite."

"In my bedside drawer," Granddad said. "Along with the diary. Now . . . read."

CHAPTER
TWENTY-FIVE

Becky munched her packet of cookies and studied the next picture. It was of some very sickly looking Germans walking toward her with their hands up. The detail was amazing. She could almost read the thoughts that were written on their faces.

"You really were an amazing artist," she said. "This picture is one of my favorites. Why didn't you paint or draw instead of create the camouflage factory when you came home?"

"Because I like to eat," Granddad said. "A no-name black artist returning from the war would have starved trying to make a living drawing or painting. Besides, getting the factory set up took every spare minute I had. Producing art that didn't have anything to do with the business was a luxury I couldn't afford."

"And afterward? After the factory was a success?"

"That's a story for another time. You're wearing me out with questions, Becky. Please start reading."

"I am certain that this war is coming to an end. I know this because when we were setting up a security perimeter last week, German soldiers saw our American soldiers and an entire group of them surrendered. It is happening to other American units, too. It's so strange to see ten or twenty Germans surrendering to one or two guards. The German troops have apparently run out of food and ammo. There is little else some of them can do except surrender.

Today I was walking outside the perimeter and there was a group of five Germans sitting on the ground with a few of our Military Police waiting to be picked up and taken to a holding area. The MPs were kind enough to give them food. As I walked by one of the German soldiers said "Good Morning" with a perfect New York accent. I stopped and said, "Good Morning" back and started a conversation with him.

It turns out that he had lived in New York for about five years as a teenager. His parents had heard the call to return to the fatherland before Hitler was seen for the crazy man he was. Then it was too late to leave Germany again and he was drafted into the German army. They could not return to America. He talked about how much he missed the hot dogs, bagels and movies. As I sat there beside of him, I learned he was no different than me. He was just a soldier doing what he had been told was best for his country. Five years ago we could have been friends.

He had not heard from his family for months, he told me, and didn't even know if his mom and dad were still alive. He thought they might be, in spite of the news he'd heard of the bombings in Berlin because they had a deep basement beneath their apartment building. As we talked, he tried to make a joke about me coming to Berlin after the war. He would show me the wonderful artwork and we could eat the food and listen to German music together.

I laughed, but my heart was not in it and neither was his. We both knew that the Berlin he remembered would not still be standing. I told him that if he happened to come to New York after the war, I would take him to a hot dog stand and buy him all he could eat. He rubbed his sunken stomach and said that I'd better have plenty of money because he had been hungry for so long he felt like he could eat every hot dog they had.

Just then a truck pulled up and the German soldiers climbed into the back with a handful of guards. The surrendering soldiers seemed so tired of war and so worn out I don't think there was enough fight in them to escape even if they'd tried.

"So one day you two were shooting at each other and the next day you were talking together like nothing had happened?" Becky asked.

"Not quite," Granddad said. "We were very aware that we had been and still were on opposite sides, but for those few minutes we allowed ourselves to simply be two men talking about better times. I don't know about him, but it was an important conversation for me. It reminded me that the German soldiers were not necessarily all evil. Some had made bad choices; some had simply become trapped in their leaders' bad decisions."

"But there were evil people involved," Becky said. "I saw some programs on TV about the concentration camps. That was evil."

"Absolutely," Granddad nodded. "There were some horribly evil people involved in that war. Our unit did not hear about the concentration camps until later and I had no idea a human could do what they did to other humans. Many German citizens did not know about the concentration camps. Many of their soldiers were just impressionable young men who followed a leader who was able to brainwash most of a nation."

"I hope I don't ever fall for something like that," Becky said.

"Becky, I doubt you would ever be fooled easily." Granddad said. "You have an inner strength and common sense that will cause you to always recognize and fight for what's right."

"Thank you," she said. "Hearing you say that makes me feel good, but I'm not sure I deserve your confidence."

"Maybe not yet," Granddad said, "but I have a feeling that after this summer you will."

"I hope you're right," Becky said. "Did you ever see that German solider again?"

"No, I didn't but when I returned after the war I spent some time in New York and whenever I saw a hot dog stand I would always look around for him. I never took a New York hot dog for granted again. I always imagined that he spent some time in a prison camp and was, hopefully, not found to have committed any war crimes. I like to think that he found his family and moved back to New York. The thing is, after you have been in a war you don't want to fight anymore. You just want people to get along and live their lives in peace."

"Do you think the Germans still hate the Jews?" Becky asked.

"Oh, there are probably small pockets of hate but very small. I did get to go back to Germany many years later. I wanted to see Berlin after The Wall came down."

CHAPTER TWENTY-FIVE

"The Wall?" Becky interrupted.

"Another long story," Granddad sighed. "Sometimes I forget how very young you are and how very old I am. I think I'll tell you about that another time, or even better— maybe you can learn about the Berlin Wall from your history teacher when you return to school this fall. But I got to meet some old German veterans like myself and their children. I asked about that question of racism and it was interesting what I learned. The children said in the best English they could use, 'We want no part of racism. We saw what it did to our country and our parents. We want nothing to do with it.' I saw in their faces that they were telling the truth. It was a small happy outcome of the war for me."

Granddad closed his eyes. "I'm sorry, Becky, but I seem to be getting tired easier these days. I think I'll take a nap."

Becky slipped the diary back into his bedside table and pulled the bed covers up over his chest. "You rest and I'll come back tomorrow."

Granddad was soon asleep. Becky sat beside his bed, mulling over what he'd said about her going back to school this fall. She hated to even think about the fall. She knew she couldn't stay here in Mississippi. Rusty and Claire had been more than kind, but she'd soon have to face the judge. Where would she live? Her spot at the foster home would be filled by now, and she didn't want to go back there anyway. Where would she go to school? It hurt to think about leaving the friends she was starting to make here. She had learned to love this small town in Mississippi. She knew it would be hard on Granddad when she left, too.

"Are you ready to go?" Rusty whispered. He tiptoed into the room when he saw that his father was asleep.

Becky glanced around the small room where her world had grown so much larger these past weeks as Granddad had told her his stories and encouraged her.

"Not really," she said, "but I'll come back tomorrow."

CHAPTER
TWENTY-SIX

It was time to begin her work on the pharmacy wall. Rusty had been able to find some scaffolding and helped her clean the wall with a steel brush and water. She had hung a heavy tarp over the wall so that she could work under it and stay out of the hot Mississippi sun. She would spend the mornings painting, but when the heat of the afternoon would hit she'd visit with Granddad in the air-conditioning. Afterwards, in the evenings when it had cooled off a little, she'd head back to her painting. One skill set Chicago had taught her was speed. Most artists would take their time but she was so used to painting and running which made her faster than most.

Of course, Mr. Troyer couldn't leave it alone and she didn't want him to. He kept bringing her water or lemonade. Emma and Mackenzie had started coming by. Sometimes they brought their parents along or other friends.

People she didn't even know started stopping by to say "Hello" and ask how her work was going. Becky only uncovered parts of the wall as she worked on it, allowing only small bits of the wall show at any given time. She hoped to be able to unveil it for Mr. Troyer's birthday which would be in a few weeks.

The longer she worked, the more she felt like she was becoming a true part of the community. Other church kids dropped by whenever they were downtown. She got so accustomed to hearing a southern drawl that she found herself saying "Y'all" without even realizing it. Mrs. Baker who ran a thrift shop across the street told her that if she tried really hard she could master the southern drawl before long.

One day Mrs. Baker's granddaughter came home from college for a visit and Mrs. Baker walked her across the street to meet Becky. When she introduced them, the older woman said, "Janie, this is Becky—You know, Rusty and Claire's girl I've been telling you about?"

Becky nearly dropped her paint brush. Had Mrs. Baker really introduced her as Rusty and Claire's girl? The feelings that suddenly washed over her were so intense she had to struggle to make small talk with Janie.

She shook it off. Rusty and Claire were doing Judge Hayes a favor. Yes, they were kind to her. Very kind. But if she thought for an instant that this good life would continue, she needed to have her head examined. Things like that only happened in books or sappy Walt Disney movies. The thing that worried her most was that the more she allowed herself to care about these people, the more it was going to hurt when she had to leave. Kind of like Claire and Rusty choosing not to adopt after their daughter died—too afraid of being hurt again.

Mrs. Baker and her granddaughter went back to the bakery and Becky trained her attention on the scene she was painting. As always, if she focused hard enough on her art, she forgot everything else. At least for a while.

A few hours later, Becky put her tools away, cleaned her hands at a backroom sink in Mr. Troyer's store, and walked the few blocks to the nursing home where Granddad was waiting for her. He wanted to hear about every detail of her painting, including the conversations she had with people on the street while she worked. She and he knew that it was an oddity in that town for a fifteen-year-old to be allowed to paint a wall, and they both wanted to make sure she knocked everyone's socks off when she revealed the completed painting.

After telling Granddad about all that had happened that morning, leaving out the way her stomach had felt when Mrs. Baker had referred to her as Rusty and Claire's girl, she pulled out the diary and turned to the page where she'd left off.

This one started with a drawing, too. It was of an odd picture and not at all like the others Granddad had drawn. It was of an airplane with question marks drawn around it and in the other corner were cross-shaped grave stones.

She was puzzled by the picture but knew the story that followed it would tell her what it was about.

It seems we sometimes fool more of our friends than our foes. Since we have to operate our unit in such secrecy it often causes confusion. We built a fake airfield this week. We had inflatable airplanes parked there and everything else that would disguise it from the air.

Imagine our surprise when all of a sudden a small army plane came in for a landing! Our guards surrounded the plane as soon as it landed and told the pilot he had to take off immediately. Of course he had a very questioning "Where am I, and what the heck did I just land in?" look.

He took off and circled low once, as though checking out what we were up to. We haven't heard that our fake air field is making the gossip rounds so I am grateful that pilot evidently knows to keep his mouth shut.

A tragedy happened recently that gives me nightmares no matter how hard I try to forget. We had set up a fake tank division to catch the attention of some Nazis who were entrenched. Our goal was to keep them in place so that our real tank divisions could swing around and surprise them.

The real tanks must not have gotten the message not to attack from around our location. All of the sudden we saw a small group of tanks bust through a forest and attack the Nazis. They must have thought we were with them and would follow and help with the attack. There were not enough of them to take on the entrenched Nazis. There was nothing, absolutely nothing we could do. We watched our fellow countrymen be slaughtered in minutes.

My heart broke thinking about the leader of those few tanks looking back wondering why we were not following, why we were not helping. He didn't understand that all we had were rubber balloons made to look like tanks. Even if we had rubber bullets we would have tried to rescue them. To our knowledge no one from that attack survived. We try not to blame ourselves. That commander reacted without thinking. He should have tried to make contact with our leadership to coordinate some sort of attack. Of course we would have prevented him from attacking. This is another part of war I just don't understand. The needless dying. Especially from lack of communication.

CHAPTER
TWENTY-SEVEN

The day had finally come. It was Mr. Troyer's birthday. Nearly the whole town had come to the town square. All the local businesses around the square had joined in the party. Snacks, balloons, and streamers lined the square. Mr. Troyer was sitting outside his drug store greeting people, making jokes, and smiling.

Becky was very nervous. Soon she would pull the sheet down and show her art. Everyone kept offering her food and drink but she knew she would not be able to keep anything down. More and more people were showing up. Becky was not ready for this. She had thought it might be maybe a dozen people or so. Instead, there were over a hundred.

Finally Mr. Troyer announced, "I'm ready for my big present."

Slowly Becky walked to the front of the crowd that

had gathered by what had once been Mr. Troyer's blank wall. Emma and Mackenzie grabbed ropes that were on either side of the canvas. They were rigged so that the sheet covering the wall would come down when the ropes were released.

Some of the other kids from her church youth group yelled, "Speech! Speech! Speech!"

Becky looked up and immediately a small group in the middle of the crowd caught her eye. There stood Rusty and Claire.

She did not expect to see Granddad in a wheelchair with a nurse behind him, nor did she expect to see Judge Hayes standing there beside him. All of them were beaming at her. She felt like her heart might explode from happiness.

Timidly, Becky made a short speech. "Mr. Troyer, all I can say is thank you for letting me use your wall as a canvas. My hope was to take something that looked like wasted space to me and turn it into something beautiful for you."

She made a gesture toward the wall and Emma and Mackenzie yanked on the rope. The sheet came down. There was a pause as everyone took in the painting, and then everyone started applauding wildly. She looked back at the crowd and her eye caught Granddad's. The look of pride on his face and the nod of affirmation he gave her meant more than the applause.

Judge Hayes and Rusty were talking and pointing to different items on the wall. Becky had attempted to capture scenes from the different veterans she'd met here in Mississippi or stories she'd heard about those who had passed on.

At the center of the mural was Mr. Troyer standing on the deck of the USS Indianapolis. There was Granddad placing a branch on a jeep hiding it from the Germans. There was Dave Reynolds who had been killed in Afghanistan defending a small village, a story his parents had told her one day while walking by. There was even a West Point scene with what was an obviously younger Rusty and Judge Hayes standing outside.

Another picture included Mrs. Troyer in the cockpit of a plane. Mr. Troyer had told Becky about his deceased wife and her service. She had flown planes from the U.S. to England over and over to support the troops. He'd given her a snapshot to copy. Another scene showed a young mother back home using rationing stamps to buy food for her family. All these scenes were superimposed upon a painted background of a giant American flag flowing in the breeze.

As Becky looked over the crowd, she felt her heart soar. She'd managed to include scenes that touched the heart of everyone there. That had been her hope, but she wasn't sure she could possibly achieve it until she saw tears streaming down the faces of some of the people who were present. It was at that moment that she knew she wasn't just some kid who liked to draw. She was an artist!

"That's my girl!" Rusty yelled.

Becky's heart leapt at his words and the pride in his voice, but she knew it would probably be the last time she would hear anything like that. She knew Judge Hayes was there to pick her up and take her back to Chicago.

After congratulations were given to her and the birthday wishes to Mr. Troyer had died down, Judge Hayes sauntered over. "Well, Becky, I see you can't stop painting on walls."

"At least you're smiling about it this time," she said.

"Isn't it better to do it with permission when it can mean something?" he asked.

"Yes," Becky said. "I never got to see the smiles of the people before. I was usually too busy running. It's nice to see people enjoy what I do." She swallowed hard. "Are you here to take me back?"

"Well, I'm still wondering what to do about that. What do you think I should do with you? I have the power to leave you here, assuming you behave yourself, or take you back and place you in foster care again."

"Foster care?" she asked. "You mean I won't have to do any time in juvie?"

"Not after what I've seen today," he said. "I'd say the community service you've provided here in this town this summer more than covers what you did back home."

"Claire and I have been talking." Rusty said, from behind her.

Becky had not realized that Rusty was listening to her conversation with the judge.

"We've been wondering if there is any way she could stay here, assuming you could work out the legalities. We've kind of been hoping she'd decide to adopt us. She's become such a part of our life that we can hardly bear the thought of parting with her."

It took a moment for what Rusty was saying to penetrate her mind. Rusty and Claire wanted her to join their family?

"Adopt you?" she said in disbelief. "You mean you want me to stay?"

"Claire and I have gotten awfully used to having a little white girl who always smells like paint hanging around our house," Rusty grinned. "It would be a shame to have that pretty room you decorated just standing there empty. We don't want to push you into something you don't want to do—but we've been hoping you'd want to stay with us."

The day turned into a blur. Accompanied by Judge Hayes, Rusty pushed Granddad's wheelchair to the office of the local judge's office. Becky didn't understand all the legal talk. She just held onto Claire's hand. What she was able to pick up was that Rusty and Claire were being given immediate guardianship over her. Becky didn't realize how tight her grip on Claire's hand was becoming until Claire said smiling, "We will never let go of you, but if you don't let some blood flow in my hand it might fall off."

At that, Becky relaxed a bit.

Finally Judge Hayes turned to Becky and said, "If you agree to this, Rusty and Claire have requested to be your guardian for now and would like to finish up adoption process, but that will take more time. You need to let Judge Bennett here know if you agree with this arrangement or n . . ."

Before he could say the word "not." Becky loudly said, "Yes!"

The adults laughed at her enthusiasm, but it was gentle laughter.

"I'm glad you feel that way about us," Rusty said.

She hugged Claire, then Rusty and then Granddad. Then she went straight for Judge Hayes. He stooped down and as she hugged him around the neck, she said in a soft voice, "Thank you for believing in me."

"Believing in you was easy," Judge Hayes said. "It was figuring out a way to help you believe in yourself that was difficult."

"Always wanted me an extra grandkid," Granddad said with a twinkle in his eye. "Never figured it would turn out to be a skinny little white girl, but I believe I'll keep her. She kinda takes after me, don't you think?"

CHAPTER
TWENTY-EIGHT

Judge Hayes stayed the night to catch up with his old friend Rusty. After supper they sat on the porch talking about their time at West Point and their fighting in Iraq. They became quiet when they would mention a soldier who had died and then laugh at some crazy stunt they or one of their friends had pulled.

Claire and Becky sat close together on the glider, listening. Every now and then Claire would reach over and smooth Becky's hair as though she could hardly believe that Becky was going to be staying with them permanently. Now that Becky knew that she would actually be living here for real and not just for the summer, she felt a peace she'd never felt before. This was a safe place and she had not known many safe places.

"By the way, Rusty," Judge Hayes said as everyone was

getting ready to go to bed. "I'd like to go spend some time with your dad tomorrow."

"Sure thing," Rusty said. "You ate at his table enough times. I'm sure he'll enjoy visiting with you."

As they followed Rusty and Claire back into the house, Judge Hayes leaned over to Becky and whispered, "I got your letter. Tomorrow, all will be made right."

Becky broke into a big smile. She hadn't been sure if Judge Hayes would pay attention to what she'd written or not. All she knew was that they might not have much time.

That night, Becky made two important phone calls before she went to sleep.

The next morning, after breakfast, they all went to go see Granddad who was happy to see Judge Hayes walk through the door. They visited for a few minutes before Mr. Troyer came into the room carrying several pink balloons.

"I heard there were some Army guys in here." He gave a show of flexing his ancient muscles. "I decided I'd bring you as manly balloons as you can handle."

Granddad and Rusty laughed and each accepted a pink balloon.

"Do you think we're ready, Becky?" Judge Hayes said.

Becky got up and looked outside the curtains which were drawn shut.

"Yes, sir. I think we are ready."

CHAPTER TWENTY-EIGHT

The others looked at each other, confused. "What are you talking about, Becky?" Claire asked.

"You'll see," Becky said as she drew back the curtain. Standing outside the ground floor window stood the entire workforce of the Camo plant. Becky slid the windows open so that the workers could hear what was happening inside.

"Is it my birthday?" Granddad asked, confused. "I thought that was still a ways off. But I've been getting more forgetful lately."

"It's not your birthday," Becky said. "It's better."

Judge Hayes cleared his throat and began to talk loudly, in what Becky recognized as his courtroom voice.

"Jared Robert Cline, it was recently brought to my attention by Becky here that due to a clerical oversight your Purple Heart was never awarded. I believe it is time for us to correct that error."

"Purple Heart?" Rusty softly interrupted, "But, Dad, I thought you always said you were just a clerk. You never said you had seen action, or that you'd been wounded."

Judge Hayes ignored Rusty and continued in his loud, authoritative voice.

"Until recently the unit and actions of Jared Robert Cline were classified. It can finally be publicly acknowledged that he was a part of the 23rd Special Troops which was a top secret unit made up of artists, magicians, and actors, who in twenty-one separate operations were credited with saving approximately 30,000 U.S. soldiers' lives by fooling the enemy to fire directly upon them instead of other troops."

"Dad?" Rusty said. "You kept this secret from us all these years?"

Granddad nodded, unable to speak. Becky saw that his chin trembled and she wondered how hard it must have been for him to keep quiet about his service all these years.

"However," Judge Hayes said, "there is another piece of the history of Jared Robert Cline that has been overlooked for too long. For injury on the beach of Normandy I am honored to be the one to give you your long overdue Purple Heart as well as a Bronze Star for meritorious service."

While saying those last words Judge Hayes pulled out two velvet cases, opened them and handed them to Granddad.

Granddad looked down at the two cases, shook his head, and said, "But there were so many other men who did greater deeds than me who deserve recognition."

He traced the two medals with his finger, as though reassuring himself that they were real. When he finally glanced up, what he saw was Mr. Troyer, Judge Hayes, Rusty, Claire, Becky and all those employees of the camo plant outside . . . standing at attention saluting him.

CHAPTER
TWENTY-NINE

It had been three years since Becky first came to Mississippi. Rusty and Claire were no longer her guardians, they were her adopted parents. No longer Claire and Rusty. She called them Mom and Dad.

Today, the three of them sat at the kitchen table looking at a lone envelope lying in the middle of the kitchen table.

"Are you going to open it?" Rusty asked. "Or will I have to?"

"Just give me a minute," Becky said nervously.

"Honey," Claire said, "no matter what it says, it does not define you or determine who you are."

Again silence. It had been a quick three years filled with growth and happiness and good memories. Becky was now eighteen and would be graduating high school soon. In her mind this envelope was her future. Everything she had worked for was either in the envelope or it was not. Finally,

Becky reached for the envelope. Her hands trembled. Again she just stared at it, fearful of the words inside that it might contain. The return address said, "West Point Academy."

Rusty put his hand on her shoulder. With that touch came generations of strength, generations of fighters. It was like her entire adopted family line was standing behind her giving their support.

Her finger slipped under the flap and it slowly opened. Again, she paused and then reached in and pulled out the paper inside. She began to read.

"Dear Ms. Rebecca Cline, Welcome to West Point class of . . ."

Before she could finish the sentence, Rusty had grabbed her, lifted her up, and hugged her so hard he nearly squeezed the breath out of her. Claire was dabbing her eyes.

"Oh, honey," Claire said. "You did it!"

It was true. With the help of God, hard work, and some good people cheering her on, she had gone from the harsh inner-city streets of Chicago to West Point—one of the most elite schools in the world. For a moment, she felt a twinge, wishing that her shadow-mother, the woman who had abandoned her—could see her now.

But that didn't matter as much to her as sharing this news with the person who meant the most to her in the world.

CHAPTER TWENTY-NINE

"I need to go see Granddad," she said.

"Go!" Rusty smiled. "He'll be so happy and proud."

She ran outside, got into the car, and drove to Granddad's. She rushed in and immediately read him the letter.

"Ah," he smiled. "My work here is done."

"Thank you." She hugged him. "Thank you for everything."

"You've done awful good for a skinny little white girl," Granddad said with a twinkle. "Now go show that school what you're made of!"

"Oh no!" Mr. Troyer, who had become Granddad's roommate, groaned dramatically and said, "Not another Army punk to deal with! You should have gotten into a real school--the Navy Academy!"

Then he smiled and put his arms out for a hug. "Congratulations! I am so proud of you."

As she walked out of the room she heard the good-natured banter of Army versus Navy by these old veterans. She did not know it then, but it would be the last time she got to speak to Granddad.

He passed away quietly that night. The nurses told her that they had found him holding the velvet boxes that contained the medals. They said there had been a peaceful look on his face.

Mr. Troyer, his long-time friend seemed to lose heart when he no longer had his old Army friend to argue with and tease. He died less than a week later.

She was devastated with the loss of Granddad, but she comforted herself with the thought that in heaven he was seeing colors like he had never seen before. His funeral was more of a celebration of a life well-lived, not a sad occasion. He left the world a better place than he had been born into. She was determined to do the same. From this moment on, she determined that she would evaluate her every action by whether or not it would make her grandfather proud.

EPILOGUE

It was only as a last resort that Special FBI Agent, Becky Cline, and her team was called into the scene. When negotiations had failed, her team and she were flown in to defuse the crisis.

This time it was Atlanta. Bank robbers were barricaded with hostages and threatening to kill them. The negotiators had been talking to them all day and night long with no progress. When hostage takers had been on edge this long they were dangerous and prone to make a very stupid decisions.

Becky's nickname was "Smoke and Mirrors." So far her rescue efforts were 100% successful. This job was going to be tricky. The bank robbers were known Islamic terrorists that had actually been trained and were good. Becky knew she was better. She was asked to try and get the robbers alive so they could be interrogated on what they were doing in the U.S. and what their plans were.

After a short briefing Becky and her team looked at the building drawings, video feeds inside and outside the bank, and looked at where the hostages were sitting. A formula started forming in her head.

Jake who was her second in command said, "Baby in a basket?"

"Just what I was thinking," Becky said. "We go at dark. Let's get set up."

Super bright lights were set up, loud speakers, some sort of small boxes were covertly placed just out of sight from where the robbers could see through the windows.

Becky knew they could pull this off, but still she knew lives were on the line. It finally got to be dark enough. Cops were visible everywhere to robbers. The robber/terrorists started to scream out insults. If Becky and her team had done their job right, everything would be over in about forty-five seconds.

Becky watched her video feeds closely. Everyone of authority was behind her keeping dead silent. Her reputation preceded her and they knew to just shut up, listen and stay out of her way.

Becky spoke in her jaw microphone. "Everyone check in."

She heard familiar voices checking in. She looked up and saw that her team was in place. They blended into the surrounding area perfectly. Her new camo outfits she helped design were working perfectly in an urban environment. She waited until it was just dark enough for the robbers' eyes to adjust to the dark because electricity had been cut to this four block area.

"Okay, team," Becky said "Baby in a basket will begin in three, two, one."

Just then a lone baby carriage was pushed into sight of the bank robbers. One of her team started screaming and running after the baby carriage like a mother who had actually lost her grip on the baby carriage.

While the robbers had an instant of confusion over "What in the world is a baby doing out here . . ."

Bam! The little boxes that had been placed out of sight exploded into sight. They were instant inflatable silhouettes of cops with guns. The robbers started opened fire on what they thought were attackers. At that instant blinding strobe lights started flashing and speakers started pulsating the most deafening sounds imaginable.

Instantly the thieves' hands went to their ears and they shut their eyes. An involuntary reaction. At that same moment her team burst through every window and door possible. Special explosives that would just knock out or daze anyone close by. A few seconds of silence and she could only see a little movement through the smoke.

"Smoke and Mirrors," her radio cracked, "Bad guys secure. Hostages shaken up a bit but zero injuries that we can see."

She looked at her watch. "Baby in a basket" had taken just under thirty-eight seconds.

Outwardl,y she was all business. Inwardly, she smiled. "Well, Granddad," she thought, "a street kid from Chicago just used art, sound, and inflatables to capture terrorists and rescue hostages with no injuries. You would be proud and I still thank God for putting you in my life."

Jake walked back into the command center and said, "We just about have everything put away. It'll soon be time to go."

"Tell the team we're going out for catfish first." She smiled. "My treat, but then I have to go straight to New York. I have a gallery opening tomorrow to prepare for."

"Your paintings?" he asked.

"Yeah," she said grinning. "My paintings."

AUTHOR'S
NOTE

It feels like I've discovered gold when I come across an unusual historical fact. The first time I read about the Ghost Army, my heart actually started beating faster. The Ghost Army really did exist and they are credited with saving over 30,000 lives. One of the most famous members of the Ghost Army was a world famous fashion designer by the name of Bill Blass. I always wondered what it was like for him to go from the foxhole to the VIP treatment of the fashion world.

The characters in the story are all fictional but they are influenced by people I know or who have passed on. Kosciusko is a real town in Mississippi and has a cute little downtown square. My favorite southern sister-in-law lives there and works at a quaint pharmacy right on the square. Kosciusko is the birth place of Oprah Winfrey. The actual structure in which she lived no longer exists but there is a sign designating the location of her home. It is amazing to think she came from such a small town.

If you ever get to Mississippi, you must try the catfish and you must have some of that amazing Blue Bell Mint Chocolate Chip Ice Cream.

MORE BOOKS
BY DEREK MILLER

FICTION:

The Attic Diary
The Kamikaze Diary

NON-FICTION:

Military Contractor's Handbook How to get Hired
... and Survive